PENGUIN BO

CHEATING AT C

LINICLA

'Stories suffused with radiant and effortless majesty; a comprehensive ease of speaking about spaces in the human heart and mind that remains out of reach for most writers' *The Times*

William Trevor was born in Mitchelstown, County Cork, and spent his childhood in provincial Ireland. He studied at Trinity College, Dublin.

He has written many novels, and has won many prizes including the Hawthornden Prize, the *Yorkshire Post* Book of the Year Award, and the Whitbread Book of the Year Award. His most recent novel, *The Story of Lucy Gault* (2002), was shortlisted for both the Man Booker Prize and the Whitbread Fiction Prize.

A celebrated short-story writer, his two most recent collections are *The Hill Bachelors* (2000), which won the Macmillan Silver Pen Award and the *Irish Times* Literature Prize, and *A Bit on the Side* (2004). Both are available in Penguin, as are his *Collected Stories*.

In 1999 William Trevor received the prestigious David Cohen Literature Prize in recognition of a lifetime's literary achievement, and in 2002 he was knighted for his services to literature.

He now lives in Devon.

# Cheating at Canasta

## WILLIAM TREVOR

PENGUIN BOOKS

PENGUIN BOOKS

Published by the Penguin Group
Penguin Books Ltd, 80 Strand, London WC2R ORL, England
Penguin Group (USA) Inc., 375 Hudson Street, New York, New York 10014, USA
Penguin Group (Canada), 90 Eglinton Avenue East, Suite 700, Toronto, Ontario, Canada M4P 2Y3
(a division of Pearson Penguin Canada Inc.)
Penguin Ireland, 25 St Stephen's Green, Dublin 2, Ireland (a division of Penguin Books Ltd)
Penguin Group (Australia), 250 Camberwell Road, Camberwell, Victoria 3124, Australia
(a division of Pearson Australia Group Pty Ltd)
Penguin Books India Pvt Ltd, 11 Community Centre, Panchsheel Park, New Delhi – 110 017, India
Penguin Group (NZ), 67 Apollo Drive, Rosedale, North Shore 0632, New Zealand
(a division of Pearson New Zealand Ltd)
Penguin Books (South Africa) (Pty) Ltd, 24 Sturdee Avenue, Rosebank, Johannesburg 2196, South Africa

Penguin Books Ltd, Registered Offices: 80 Strand, London WC2R ORL, England

www.penguin.com

First published by Viking 2007
Published in Penguin Books 2008

2

These stories were first published in the *Guardian*, the *New Yorker*,
the *Sewanee Review* and *Tatler*

Typeset by Rowland Phototypesetting Ltd, Bury St Edmunds, Suffolk
Printed in England by Clays Ltd, St Ives plc

ISBN: 978-0-141-03245-0

www.greenpenguin.co.uk

Penguin Books is committed to a sustainable future
for our business, our readers and our planet.
The book in your hands is made from paper
certified by the Forest Stewardship Council.

# Contents

# The Dressmaker's Child

Cahal sprayed WD-40 on to the only bolt his spanner wouldn't shift. All the others had come out easily enough but this one was rusted in, the exhaust unit trailing from it. He had tried to hammer it out, he had tried wrenching the exhaust unit this way and that in the hope that something would give way, but nothing had. Half five, he'd told Heslin, and the bloody car wouldn't be ready.

The lights of the garage were always on because shelves had been put up in front of the windows that stretched across the length of the wall at the back. Abandoned cars, kept for their parts, and cars and motor-cycles waiting for spares, and jacks that could be wheeled about, took up what space there was on either side of the small wooden office, which was at the back also. There were racks of tools, and workbenches with vices along the back wall, and rows of new and reconditioned tyres, and drums of grease and oil. In the middle of the garage there were two pits, in one of which Cahal's father was at the moment, putting in a clutch. There was a radio on which advice was being given about looking after fish in an aquarium. 'Will you turn that stuff off?' Cahal's father shouted from under the car he was working on, and Cahal searched the wavebands until he found music of his father's time.

He was an only son in a family of girls, all of them

older, all of them gone from the town – three to England, another in Dunne's in Galway, another married in Nebraska. The garage was what Cahal knew, having kept his father company there since childhood, given odd jobs to do as he grew up. His father had had help then, an old man who was related to the family, whose place Cahal eventually took.

He tried the bolt again but the WD-40 hadn't begun to work yet. He was a lean, almost scrawny youth, dark-haired, his long face usually unsmiling. His garage overalls, over a yellow T-shirt, were oil-stained, gone pale where their green dye had been washed out of them. He was nineteen years old.

'Hullo,' a voice said. A man and a woman, strangers, stood in the wide open doorway of the garage.

'Howya,' Cahal said.

'It's the possibility, sir,' the man enquired, 'you drive us to the sacred Virgin?'

'Sorry?' And Cahal's father shouted up from the pit, wanting to know who was there. 'Which Virgin's that?' Cahal asked.

The two looked at one another, not attempting to answer, and it occurred to Cahal that they were foreign people, who had not understood. A year ago a German had driven his Volkswagen into the garage, with a noise in the engine, so he'd said. 'I had hopes it'd be the big end,' Cahal's father admitted afterwards, but it was only the catch of the bonnet gone a bit loose. A couple from America had had a tyre put on their hired car a few weeks after that, but there'd been nothing since.

'Of Pouldearg,' the woman said. 'Is it how to say it?'

'The statue you're after?'

They nodded uncertainly and then with more confidence, both of them at the same time.

'Aren't you driving, yourselves, though?' Cahal asked them.

'We have no car,' the man said.

'We are travelled from Ávila.' The woman's black hair was silky, drawn back and tied with a red and blue ribbon. Her eyes were brown, her teeth very white, her skin olive. She wore the untidy clothes of a traveller: denim trousers, a woollen jacket over a striped red blouse. The man's trousers were the same, his shirt a nondescript shade of greyish blue, a white kerchief at his neck. A few years older than himself, Cahal estimated they'd be.

'Ávila?' he said.

'Spain,' the man said.

Again Cahal's father called out, and Cahal said two Spanish people had come into the garage.

'In the store,' the man explained. 'They say you drive us to the Virgin.'

'Are they broken down?' Cahal's father shouted.

He could charge them fifty euros, Pouldearg there and back, Cahal considered. He'd miss Germany versus Holland on the television, maybe the best match of the Cup, but never mind that for fifty euros.

'The only thing,' he said, 'I have an exhaust to put in.'

He pointed at the pipe and silencer hanging out of Heslin's old Vauxhall, and they understood. He gestured with his hands that they should stay where they were for a minute, and with his palms held flat made a pushing motion in the air, indicating that they should ignore the agitation that was coming from the pit. Both of them were amused. When Cahal tried the bolt again it began to turn.

He made the thumbs-up sign when exhaust and silencer clattered to the ground. 'I could take you at around seven,' he said, going close to where the Spaniards stood, keeping his voice low so that his father would not hear. He led them to the forecourt and made the arrangement while he filled the tank of a Murphy's Stout lorry.

\*

When he'd driven a mile out on the Ennis road, Cahal's father turned at the entrance to the stud farm and drove back to the garage, satisfied that the clutch he'd put in for Father Shea was correctly adjusted. He left the car on the forecourt, ready for Father Shea to collect, and hung the keys up in the office. Heslin from the court-house was writing a cheque for the exhaust Cahal had fitted. Cahal was getting out of his overalls, and when Heslin had gone he said the people who had come wanted him to drive them to Pouldearg. They were Spanish people, Cahal said again, in case his father hadn't heard when he'd supplied that information before.

'What they want with Pouldearg?'

'Nothing only the statue.'

'There's no one goes to the statue these times.'

'It's where they're headed.'

'Did you tell them, though, how the thing was?'

'I did of course.'

'Why they'd be going out there?'

'There's people takes photographs of it.'

Thirteen years ago, the then bishop and two parish priests had put an end to the cult of the wayside statue at Pouldearg. None of those three men, and no priest or nun who had ever visited the crossroads at Pouldearg, had sensed anything special about the statue; none had witnessed the tears that were said to slip out of the downcast eyes when pardon for sins was beseeched by penitents. The statue became the subject of attention in pulpits and in religious publications, the claims made for it fulminated against as a foolishness. And then a curate of that time demonstrated that what had been noticed by two or three local people who regularly passed by the statue – a certain dampness beneath the eyes – was no more than raindrops trapped in two over-defined hollows. There the matter ended. Those who had so certainly believed in what they had never actually seen, those who had not noticed the drenched leaves of over-hanging boughs high above the statue, felt as foolish as their spiritual masters had predicted they one day would. Almost overnight the weeping Virgin of Pouldearg became again the painted image it had always been. Our Lady of the Wayside, it had been called for a while.

'I never heard people were taking photographs of it.' Cahal's father shook his head as if he doubted his son, which he often did and usually with reason.

'A fellow was writing a book a while back. Going around all Ireland, tracking down the weeping statues.'

'It was no more than the rain at Pouldearg.'

'He'd have put that in the book. That man would have put the whole thing down, how you'd find the statues all over the place and some of them would be okay and some of them wouldn't.'

'And you set the Spaniards right about Pouldearg?'

'I did of course.'

'Drain the juice out of young Leahy's bike and we'll weld his leak for him.'

★

The suspicions of Cahal's father were justified: the truth had no more than slightly played a part in what Cahal had told the Spanish couple about Pouldearg. With fifty euros at the back of his mind, he would have considered it a failure of his intelligence had he allowed himself to reveal that the miracle once claimed for the statue at Pouldearg was without foundation. They had heard the statue called Our Lady of Tears as well as Our Lady of the Wayside and the Sacred Virgin of Pouldearg by a man in a Dublin public house with whom they had drifted into conversation. They'd had to repeat this a couple of times before Cahal grasped what they were saying, but he thought he got it right in the end. It wouldn't be hard to stretch the journey by four or five miles, and if they were misled by the names they'd heard the statue given in Dublin it was no concern of his. At five past seven, when he'd had his tea and had had a look at the television, he drove into the yard of Macey's Hotel. He waited there as he'd said he would. They appeared almost at once.

They sat close together in the back. Before he started the engine again Cahal told them what the cost would be and they said that was all right. He drove through the town, gone quiet as it invariably did at this time. Some of the shops were still open and would remain so for a few more hours – the newsagents' and tobacconists', the sweet shops and small groceries, Quinlan's supermarket, all the public houses – but there was a lull on the streets.

'Are you on holiday?' Cahal asked.

He couldn't make much of their reply. Both of them spoke, correcting one another. After a lot of repetition they seemed to be telling him that they were getting married.

'Well, that's grand,' he said.

He turned out on to the Loye road. Spanish was spoken in the back of the car. The radio wasn't working or he'd have put it on for company. The car was a black Ford Cortina with a hundred and eighty thousand miles on the clock; his father had taken it in part-exchange. They'd use it until the tax disc expired and then put it aside for spares. Cahal thought of telling them that in case they'd think he hadn't much to say for himself, but he knew it would be too difficult. The Christian Brothers had had him labelled as not having much to say for himself, and it had stuck in his memory, worrying him sometimes in case it caused people to believe he was slow. Whenever he could, Cahal tried to give the lie to that by making a comment.

'Are you here long?' he enquired, and the girl said they'd been two days in Dublin. He said he'd been in Dublin himself a few times. He said it was mountainy from now on, until they reached Pouldearg. The scenery was beautiful, the girl said.

He took the fork at the two dead trees, although going straight would have got them there too, longer still but potholes all over the place. It was a good car for the hills, the man said, and Cahal said it was a Ford, pleased that he'd understood. You'd get used to it, he considered; with a bit more practising you'd pick up the trick of understanding them.

'How'd you say it in Spanish?' he called back over his shoulder. 'A statue?'

'*Estatua*,' they both said, together. '*Estatua*,' they said.

'*Estatua*,' Cahal repeated, changing gear for the hill at Loye.

The girl clapped her hands, and he could see her smiling in the driving mirror. God, a woman like that, he thought. Give me a woman like that, he said to himself, and he imagined he was in the car alone with her, that the man wasn't there, that he hadn't come to Ireland with her, that he didn't exist.

'Do you hear about St Teresa of Ávila? Do you hear about her in Ireland?' Her lips opened and closed in the driving mirror, her teeth flashing, the tip of her tongue there for a moment. What she'd asked him was as clear as anyone would say it.

'We do, of course,' he said, confusing St Teresa of Ávila with the St Teresa who'd been famous for her humility and her attention to little things. 'Grand,' Cahal attributed to her also. 'Grand altogether.'

To his disappointment, Spanish was spoken again. He was going with Minnie Fennelly, but no doubt about it this woman had the better of her. The two faces appeared side by side in his mind's eye and there wasn't a competition. He drove past the cottages beyond the bridge, the road twisting and turning all over the place after that. It said earlier on the radio there'd be showers but there wasn't a trace of one, the October evening without a breeze, dusk beginning.

'Not more than a mile,' he said, not turning his head, but the Spanish was still going on. If they were planning to take photographs they mightn't be lucky by the time they got there. With the trees, Pouldearg was a dark place at the best of times. He wondered if the Germans had scored yet. He'd have put money on the Germans if he'd had any to spare.

Before they reached their destination Cahal drew the car on to the verge where it was wide and looked dry. He could tell from the steering that there was trouble and found it in the front offside wheel, the tyre leaking at the valve. Five or six pounds it would have lost, he estimated.

'It won't take me a minute,' he reassured his passengers, rummaging behind where they sat, among old newspapers and tools and empty paint tins, for the pump. He thought for a moment it mightn't be there and wondered what he'd do if the spare tyre was flat, which sometimes it was if a car was a trade-in. But the pump was there and he gave the partially deflated tyre a couple of extra pounds to keep it going. He'd see how things were when they reached Pouldearg crossroads.

When they did, there wasn't enough light for a photograph, but the two went up close to the Wayside Virgin, which was more lopsided than Cahal remembered it from the last time he'd driven by it, hardly longer than a year ago. The tyre had lost the extra pressure he'd pumped in and while they were occupied he began to change the wheel, having discovered that the spare tyre wasn't flat. All the time he could hear them talking in Spanish, although their voices weren't raised. When they returned to the car it was still jacked up and they had to wait for a while, standing on the road beside him, but they didn't appear to mind.

He'd still catch most of the second half, Cahal said to himself when eventually he turned the car and began the journey back. You never knew how you were placed as regards how long you'd be, how long you'd have to wait for people while they poked about.

'Was she all right for you?' he asked them, turning on the headlights so that the potholes would show up.

They answered in Spanish, as if they had forgotten that it wouldn't be any good. She'd fallen over a bit more, he said, but they didn't understand. They brought up the man they'd met in the public house in Dublin. They kept repeating something, a gabble of English words that still appeared to be about getting married. In the end, it seemed to Cahal that this man had told them people received a marriage blessing when they came to Pouldearg as penitents.

'Did you buy him drinks?' he asked, but that wasn't understood either.

They didn't meet another car, nor even a bicycle until they were further down. He'd been lucky over the tyre: they could easily have said they wouldn't pay if he'd had them stranded all night in the hills. They weren't talking any more; when he looked in the mirror they were kissing, no more than shadows in the gloom, arms around one another.

It was then, just after they'd passed the dead trees, that the child ran out. She came out of the blue cottage and ran at the car. He'd heard of it before, the child on this road who ran out at cars. It had never happened to himself, he'd never even seen a child there any time he'd passed, but often it was mentioned. He felt the thud no more than a second after the headlights picked out the white dress by the wall and then the sudden movement of the child running out.

Cahal didn't stop. In his mirror the road had gone dark again. He saw something white lying there but said to himself he had imagined it. In the back of the Cortina the embrace continued.

Sweat had broken on the palms of Cahal's hands, on his back and his forehead. She'd thrown herself at the side of the car and his own door was what she'd made contact with. Her mother was the unmarried woman of that cottage, many the time he'd heard that said in the garage. Fitzie Gill had shown him damage to his wing and said the child must have had a stone in her hand. But usually there wasn't any damage, and no one had ever mentioned damage to the child herself.

Bungalows announced the town, all of them lit up now. The Spanish began again, and he was asked if he could tell them what time the bus went to Galway. There was confusion because he thought they meant tonight, but then he understood it was the morning. He told them and when they paid him in Macey's yard the man handed him a pencil and a notebook. He didn't know what that was for, but they showed him, making gestures, and he wrote down the time of the bus. They shook hands with him before they went into the hotel.

★

In the very early morning, just after half past one, Cahal woke up and couldn't sleep again. He tried to recall what he'd seen of the football, the moves there'd been, the saves, the yellow card shown twice. But nothing seemed quite right, as if the television pictures and snatches of the commentary came from a dream, which he knew they hadn't. He had examined the side of the car in the garage and there'd been nothing. He had switched out the lights of the garage and locked up. He'd watched the football in Shannon's and hadn't seen the end because he lost interest when nothing much was happening. He should have stopped; he didn't know why he hadn't. He couldn't remember braking. He didn't know if he'd tried to, he didn't know if there hadn't been time.

The Ford Cortina had been seen setting out on the Loye road, and then returning. His father knew the way he'd gone, past the unmarried woman's cottage. The Spaniards would have said in the hotel they'd seen the Virgin. They'd have said in the hotel they were going on to Galway. They could be found in Galway for questioning.

In the dark Cahal tried to work it out. They would have heard the bump. They wouldn't have known what it was, but they'd have heard it while they were kissing one another. They would remember how much longer it was before they got out of the car in Macey's yard. It hadn't been a white dress, Cahal realized suddenly: it trailed on the ground, too long for a dress, more like a nightdress.

He'd seen the woman who lived there a few times when she came in to the shops, a dressmaker they said she was, small and wiry with dark inquisitive eyes and a twist in her features that made them less appealing than they might have been. When her child had been born to her the father had not been known – not even to herself, so it was said, though possibly without justification. People said she didn't speak about the birth of her child.

As Cahal lay in the darkness, he resisted the compulsion to get up in order to go back and see for himself; to walk out to the blue cottage, since to drive would be foolish; to look on the road for whatever might be there, he didn't know what. Often he and Minnie Fennelly got up in the middle of the night in order to meet in the back shed at her house. They lay on a stack of netting there, whispering and petting one another, the way they couldn't anywhere in the daytime. The best they could manage in the daytime was half an hour in the Ford Cortina out in the country somewhere. They could spend half the night in the shed.

He calculated how long it would take him to walk out to where the incident had occurred. He wanted to; he wanted to get there and see nothing on the road and to close his eyes in relief. Sometimes dawn had come by the time he parted from Minnie Fennelly, and he imagined that too, the light beginning as he walked in from the country feeling all right again. But more likely he wouldn't be.

'One day that kid'll be killed,' he heard Fitzie Gill saying, and someone else said the woman wasn't up to looking after the kid. The child was left alone in the house, people said, even for a night while the woman drank by herself in Leahy's, looking around for a man to keep her company.

That night, Cahal didn't sleep again. And all the next day he waited for someone to walk into the garage and say what had been found. But no one did, and no one did the next day either, or the day after that. The Spaniards would have gone on from Galway by now, the memories of people who had maybe noticed the Ford Cortina would be getting shaky. And Cahal counted the drivers whom he knew for a fact had experienced similar incidents with the child and said to himself that maybe, after all, he'd been fortunate. Even so, it would be a long time before he drove past that cottage again, if ever he did.

Then something happened that changed all that. Sitting

with Minnie Fennelly in the Cyber Café one evening, Minnie Fennelly said, 'Don't look, only someone's staring at you.'

'Who is it?'

'D'you know that dressmaker woman?'

They'd ordered chips and they came just then. Cahal didn't say anything, but knew that sooner or later he wasn't going to be able to prevent himself from looking around. He wanted to ask if the woman had her child with her, but in the town he had only ever seen her on her own and he knew that the child wouldn't be there. If she was it would be a chance in a thousand, he thought, the apprehension that had haunted him on the night of the incident flooding his consciousness, stifling everything else.

'God, that one gives me the creeps!' Minnie Fennelly muttered, splashing vinegar on to her chips.

Cahal looked round them. He caught a glimpse of the dressmaker, alone, before he quickly looked back. He could still feel her eyes on his back. She would have been in Leahy's; the way she was sitting suggested drunkenness. When they'd finished their chips and the coffee they'd been brought while they were waiting, he asked if she was still there.

'She is, all right. D'you know her? Does she come into the garage?'

'Ah no, she hasn't a car. She doesn't come in.'

'I'd best be getting back, Cahal.'

He didn't want to go yet, while the woman was there. But if they waited they could be here for hours. He didn't want to pass near her, but as soon as he'd paid and stood up he saw they'd have to. When they did she spoke to Minnie Fennelly, not him.

'Will I make your wedding-dress for you?' the dressmaker offered. 'Would you think of me at all when it'll be the time you'd want it?'

And Minnie Fennelly laughed and said no way they were ready for wedding-dresses yet.

'Cahal knows where he'll find me,' the dressmaker said. 'Amn't I right, Cahal?'

'I thought you didn't know her,' Minnie Fennelly said when they were outside.

*

Three days after that, Mr Durcan left his pre-war Riley in because the hand-brake was slipping. He'd come back for it at four, he arranged, and said before he left: 'Did you hear that about the dressmaker's child?'

He wasn't the kind to get things wrong. Fussy, with a thin black moustache, his Riley sports the pride of his bachelor life, he was as tidy in what he said as he was in how he dressed.

'Gone missing,' he said now. 'The gardaí are in on it.'

It was Cahal's father who was being told this. Cahal, with the cooling system from Gibney's bread van in pieces on a workbench, had just found where the tube had perished.

'She's backward, the child,' his father said.

'She is.'

'You hear tales.'

'She's gone off for herself anyway. They have a block on a couple of roads, asking was she seen.'

The unease that hadn't left him since the dressmaker had been in the Cyber Café began to nag again when Cahal heard that. He wondered what questions the gardaí were asking; he wondered when it was that the child had taken herself off; although he tried, he couldn't piece anything together.

'Isn't she a backward woman herself, though?' his father remarked when Mr Durcan had gone. 'Sure, did she ever lift a finger to tend that child?'

Cahal didn't say anything. He tried to think about marrying Minnie Fennelly, although still nothing was fixed, not even an agreement between themselves. Her plump honest features became vivid for a moment in his consciousness, the same plumpness in her arms and her hands. He found it attractive, he always had, since first he'd noticed her when she was still going to the nuns. He shouldn't have had thoughts about the Spanish girl, he shouldn't have let himself. He should have told them the statue was nothing, that the man they'd met had been pulling a fast one for the sake of the drinks they'd buy him.

'Your mother had that one run up curtains for the back room,' his father said. 'Would you remember that, boy?'

Cahal shook his head.

'Ah, you wouldn't have been five at the time, maybe younger yet. She was just after setting up with the dress-making, her father still there in the cottage with her. The priests said give her work on account she was a charity. Bedad, they wouldn't say it now!'

Cahal turned the radio on and turned the volume up. Madonna was singing, and he imagined her in the get-up she'd fancied for herself a few years ago, suspenders and items of underclothes. He'd thought she was great.

'I'm taking the Toyota out,' his father said, and the bell from the forecourt rang, someone waiting there for petrol. It didn't concern him, Cahal told himself as he went to answer it. What had occurred on the evening of Germany and Holland was a different thing altogether from the news Mr Durcan had brought, no way could it be related.

'Howya,' he greeted the school-bus driver at the pumps.

\*

The dressmaker's child was found where she'd lain for several days, at the bottom of a fissure, partly covered with shale, in the exhausted quarry half a mile from where she'd lived. Years ago the last of the stone had been carted away and a barbed-wire fence put up, with two warning notices about danger. She would have crawled in under the bottom strand of wire, the gardaí said, and a chain-link fence replaced the barbed wire within a day.

In the town the dressmaker was condemned, blamed behind her back for the tragedy that had occurred. That her own father, who had raised her on his own since her mother's early death, had himself been the father of the child was an ugly calumny, not voiced before, but seeming now to have a natural place in the paltry existence of a child who had lived and died wretchedly.

'How are you, Cahal?' Cahal heard the voice of the dressmaker behind him when, early one November morning, he made his way to the shed where he and Minnie Fennelly indulged their affection for one another. It was not yet one o'clock, the town lights long ago extinguished except for a few in Main Street. 'Would you come home with me, Cahal? Would we walk out to where I am?'

All this was spoken to his back while Cahal walked on. He knew who was there. He knew who it was, he didn't have to look.

'Leave me alone,' he said.

'Many's the night I rest myself on the river seat and many's the night I see you. You'd always be in a hurry, Cahal.'

'I'm in a hurry now.'

'One o'clock in the morning! Arrah, go on with you, Cahal!'

'I don't know you. I don't want to be talking to you.'

'She was gone for five days before I went to the guards. It wouldn't be the first time she was gone off. A minute wouldn't go by without she was out on the road.'

Cahal didn't say anything. Even though he still didn't turn round he could smell the drink on her, stale and acrid.

'I didn't go to them any quicker for fear they'd track down the way it was when the lead would be fresh for them. D'you understand me, Cahal?'

Cahal stopped. He turned round and she almost walked into him. He told her to go away.

'The road was the thing with her. First thing of a morning she'd be running at the cars without a pick of food inside her. The next thing is she'd be off up the road to the statue. She'd kneel to the statue the whole day until she was found by some old fellow who'd bring her back to me. Some old fellow'd have her by the hand and they'd walk in the door. Oh, many's the time, Cahal. Wasn't it the first place the guards looked when I said that to the sergeant? Any woman'd do her best for her own, Cahal.'

'Will you leave me alone!'

'Gone seven it was, maybe twenty past. I had the door open to go into Leahy's and I seen the black car going by and yourself inside it. You always notice a car in the evening time, only the next thing was I was late back from Leahy's and she was gone. D'you understand me, Cahal?'

'It's nothing to do with me.'

'He'd have gone back the same way he went out, I said to myself, but I didn't mention it to the guards, Cahal. Was she in the way of wandering in her nightdress? was what they asked me and I told them she'd be out the door before you'd see her. Will we go home, Cahal?'

'I'm not going anywhere with you.'

'There'd never be a word of blame on yourself, Cahal.'

'There's nothing to blame me for. I had people in the car that evening.'

'I swear before God, what's happened is done with. Come back with me now, Cahal.'

'Nothing happened, nothing's done with. There was Spanish people in the car the entire time. I drove them out to Pouldearg and back again to Macey's Hotel.'

'Minnie Fennelly's no use to you, Cahal.'

He had never seen the dressmaker close before. She was younger than he'd thought, but still looked a fair bit older than himself, maybe twelve or thirteen years. The twist in her face wasn't ugly, but it spoilt what might have been beauty of a kind, and he remembered the flawless beauty of the Spanish girl and the silkiness of her hair. The dressmaker's hair was black too, but wild and matted, limply straggling, falling to her shoulders. The eyes that had stared so intensely at him in the Cyber Café were bleary. Her full lips were drawn back in a smile, one of her teeth slightly chipped. Cahal walked away and she did not follow him.

That was the beginning; there was no end. In the town, though never again at night, she was always there: Cahal knew that was an illusion, that she wasn't always there but seemed so because her presence on each occasion meant so much. She tidied herself up; she wore dark clothes, which people said were in mourning for her child; and people said she had ceased to frequent Leahy's public house. She was seen painting the front of her cottage, the same blue shade, and tending its bedraggled front garden. She walked from the shops of the town, and never now stood, hand raised, in search of a lift.

Continuing his familiar daily routine of repairs and

servicing and answering the petrol bell, Cahal found himself unable to dismiss the connection between them that the dressmaker had made him aware of when she'd walked behind him in the night, and knew that the roots it came from spread and gathered strength and were nurtured, in himself, by fear. Cahal was afraid without knowing what he was afraid of, and when he tried to work this out he was bewildered. He began to go to Mass and to confession more often than he ever had before. It was noticed by his father that he had even less to say these days to the customers at the pumps or when they left their cars in. His mother wondered about his being anaemic and put him on iron pills. Returning occasionally to the town for a couple of days at a weekend, his sister who was still in Ireland said the trouble must surely be to do with Minnie Fennelly.

During all this time – passing in other ways quite normally – the child was lifted again and again from the cleft in the rocks, still in her nightdress as Cahal had seen her, laid out and wrapped as the dead are wrapped. If he hadn't had to change the wheel he would have passed the cottage at a different time and the chances were she wouldn't have been ready to run out, wouldn't just then have felt inclined to. If he'd explained to the Spaniards about the Virgin's tears being no more than rain he wouldn't have been on the road at all.

The dressmaker did not speak to him again or seek to, but he knew that the fresh blue paint, and the mourning clothes that were not, with time, abandoned, and the flowers that came to fill the small front garden, were all for him. When a little more than a year had passed since the evening he'd driven the Spanish couple out to Pouldearg, he attended Minnie Fennelly's wedding when she married Des Downey, a vet from Athenry.

The dressmaker had not said it, but it was what there had been between them in the darkened streets: that he had gone back, walking out as he had wanted to that night when he'd lain awake, that her child had been there where she had fallen on the road, that he had carried her to the quarry. And Cahal knew it was the dressmaker, not he, who had done that.

He visited the Virgin of the Wayside, always expecting that she might be there. He knelt, and asked for nothing. He spoke only in his thoughts, offering reparation and promising to accept whatever might be visited upon him for associating himself with the mockery of the man the Spaniards had met by chance in Dublin, for mocking the lopsided image on the road, taking fifty euros for a lie. He had looked at them kissing. He had thought about Madonna with her clothes off, not minding that she called herself that.

Once when he was at Pouldearg, Cahal noticed the glisten of what had once been taken for tears on the Virgin's cheek. He touched the hollow where this moisture had accumulated and raised his dampened finger to his lips. It did not taste of salt, but that made no difference. Driving back, when he went by the dressmaker's blue cottage she was there in the front garden, weeding her flowerbeds. Even though she didn't look up, he wanted to go to her and knew that one day he would.

# The Room

'Do you know why you are doing this?' he asked, and Katherine hesitated, then shook her head, although she did know.

Nine years had almost healed a soreness, each day made a little easier, until the balm of work was taken from her and in her scratchy idleness the healing ceased. She was here because of that, there was no other reason she could think of, but she didn't say it.

'And you?' she asked instead.

He was forthcoming, or sounded so; he'd been attracted by her at a time when he'd brought loneliness upon himself by quarrelling once too often with the wife who had borne his children and had cared for him.

'I'm sorry about the room,' he said.

His belongings were piled up, books and cardboard boxes, suitcases open, not yet unpacked. A word-processor had not been plugged in, its flexes trailing on the floor. Clothes on hangers cluttered the back of the door, an anatomical study of an elephant decorated one of the walls, with arrows indicating where certain organs were beneath the leathery skin. This grey picture wasn't his, he'd said when Katherine asked; it came with the room, which was all he had been able to find in a hurry. A sink was in the same corner as a wash-basin, an electric kettle and a gas-ring on a shelf, a green plastic curtain not drawn across.

'It's all a bit more special now that you're here,' he said.

When she got up to put on her clothes, Katherine could tell he didn't want her to go. Yet he, not she, was the one who had to; she could have stayed all afternoon. Buttoning a sleeve of her dress, she remarked that at least she knew now what it felt like to deceive.

'What it had felt like for Phair,' she said.

She pulled the edge of the curtain back a little so that the light fell more directly on the room's single looking-glass. She tidied her hair, still brown, no grey in it yet. Her mother's hadn't gone grey at all, and her grandmother's only when she was very old, which was something Katherine hoped she wouldn't have to be; she was forty-seven now. Her dark eyes gazed back at her from her reflection, her lipstick smudged, an emptiness in her features that had not to do with the need to renew her makeup. Her beauty was ebbing – but slowly, and there was beauty left.

'You were curious about that?' he asked. 'Deception?'

'Yes, I was curious.'

'And shall you be again?'

Still settling the disturbances in her face, Katherine didn't answer at once. Then she said: 'If you would like me to.'

Outside, the afternoon was warm, the street where the room was – above a betting shop – seemed brighter and more gracious than Katherine had noticed when she'd walked the length of it earlier. There was an after-noon tranquillity about it in spite of shops and cars. The tables were unoccupied outside the Prince and Dog, hanging baskets of petunias on either side of its regal figure and a Dalmatian with a foot raised. There was a Costa Coffee next to a Prêt à Manger and Katherine crossed to it. '*Latte*,' she ordered from the girls who were operating the Gaggia machines, and picked out a florentine from the glass case on the counter while she waited for it.

She hardly knew the man she'd slept with. He'd danced with her at a party she'd gone to alone, and then he'd danced with her again, holding her closer, asking her her name and giving his. Phair didn't accompany her to parties these days and she didn't go often herself. But she'd known what she intended, going to this one.

The few tables were all taken. She found a stool at the bar that ran along one of the walls. *Teenagers' Curfew!* a headline in someone else's evening paper protested, a note of indignation implied, and for a few moments she wondered what all that was about and then lost interest.

Phair would be quietly at his desk, in shirtsleeves, the blue-flecked shirt she'd ironed the day before yesterday, his crinkly, gingerish hair as it had been that morning when he left the house, his agreeable smile welcoming anyone who approached him. In spite of what had happened nine years ago, Phair had not been made redundant, that useful euphemism for being sacked. That he'd been kept on was a tribute to his success in the past, and of course it wasn't done to destroy a man when he was down. 'We should go away,' she'd said, and remembered saying it now, but he hadn't wanted to, because running away was something that wasn't done either. He would have called it running away, in fact he had.

This evening he would tell her about his day, and she would say about hers and would have to lie. And in turn they'd listen while she brought various dishes to the dining-table, and he would pour her wine. None for himself because he didn't drink any more, unless someone pressed him and then only in order not to seem ungracious. 'My marriage is breaking up,' the man who'd made love to her in his temporary accommodation had confided when, as strangers, they had danced together. 'And yours?' he'd asked, and she'd hesitated and then said no, not breaking up. There'd never been talk of that. And when they danced the second time, after they'd had a drink together and then a few more, he asked her if she had children and she said she hadn't. That she was not able to had been known before the marriage and then become part of it – as her employment at the Charterhouse Institute had been until six weeks ago, when the Institute had decided to close itself down.

'Idleness is upsetting,' she had said while they danced, and had asked the man who held her closer now if he had ever heard of Sharon Ritchie. People often thought they hadn't and then remembered. He shook his head and the name was still unfamiliar to him when she told him why it might not have been. 'Sharon Ritchie was murdered,' she'd said, and wouldn't have without the few drinks. 'My husband was accused.'

She blew on the surface of her coffee but it was still

too hot. She tipped sugar out of its paper spill into her teaspoon and watched the sugar darkening when the coffee soaked it. She loved the taste of that, as much a pleasure as anything there'd been this afternoon. 'Oh, suffocated,' she'd said, when she'd been asked how the person called Sharon Ritchie had died. 'She was suffocated with a cushion.' Sharon Ritchie had had a squalid life, living grandly at a good address, visited by many men.

Katherine sat a while longer, staring at the crumbs of her florentine, her coffee drunk. 'We live with it,' she had said when they left the party together, he to return to the wife he didn't get on with, she to the husband whose deceiving of her had ended with a death. Fascinated by what was lived with, an hour ago in the room that was his temporary accommodation her afternoon lover had wanted to know everything.

On the Tube she kept seeing the room: the picture of the elephant, the suitcases, the trailing flexes, the clothes on the back of the door. Their voices echoed, his curiosity, her evasions and then telling a little more because, after all, she owed him something. 'He paid her with a cheque once, oh ages ago. That was how they brought him into things. And when they talked to the old woman in the flat across the landing from Sharon Ritchie's she recognised him in the photograph she was shown. Oh yes, we live with it.'

Her ticket wouldn't operate the turnstile when she tried to leave the Tube station and she remembered that she had guessed how much the fare should be and must have got it wrong. The Indian who was there to deal with such errors was inclined to be severe. Her journey had been different earlier, she tried to explain; she'd got things muddled. 'Well, these things happen,' the Indian said, and she realized his severity had not been meant. When she smiled he didn't notice. That is his way too, she thought.

She bought two chicken breasts, free-range, organic; and courgettes and Medjool dates. She hadn't made a list as she usually did, and wondered if this had to do with the kind of afternoon it had been and thought it probably had. She tried to remember which breakfast cereals needed to be replenished but couldn't. And then remembered Normandy butter, and Braeburns and tomatoes. It was just before five o'clock when she let herself into the flat. The telephone was ringing and Phair said he'd be a bit late, not by much, maybe twenty minutes. She ran a bath.

\*

The tips of his fingers stroked the arm that was close to him. He said he thought he loved her. Katherine shook her head.

'Tell me,' he said.

'I have, though.'

He didn't press it. They lay in silence for a while. Then Katherine said: 'I love him more, now that I feel so sorry for him too. He pitied me when I knew I was to be deprived of the children we both wanted. Love makes the most of pity, or pity does of love, I don't know which. It hardly matters.'

She told him more, and realized she wanted to, which she hadn't known before. When the two policemen had come in the early morning she had not been dressed. Phair was making coffee. 'Phair Alexander Warburton,' one of them had said. She'd heard him from the bedroom, her bath water still gurgling out. She'd thought they'd come to report a death, as policemen sometimes have to: her mother's or Phair's aunt, who was his next of kin. When she went downstairs they were talking about the death of someone whose name she did not know. 'Who?' she asked, and the taller of the two policemen said Sharon Ritchie and Phair said nothing.

'Your husband has explained,' the other man said, 'that you didn't know Miss Ritchie.' A Thursday night, the eighth, two weeks ago, they said: what time – could she remember – had her husband come in?

She'd faltered, lost in all this. 'But who's this person? Why are you here?' And the taller policeman said there were a few loose ends. 'Sit down, madam,' his colleague put in and she was asked again what time her husband had come in. The usual misery on the Northern line, he'd said that night, the Thursday before last. He'd given up on it, as everyone else was doing, then hadn't been able to get a taxi because of the rain. 'You remember, madam?' the taller policeman prompted, and something made her say the usual time. She couldn't think; she couldn't because she was trying to remember if Phair had ever mentioned Sharon Ritchie. 'Your husband visited Miss

Ritchie,' the same policeman said, and the other man's pager sounded and he took it to the window, turning his back to them.

'No, we're talking to him now,' he mumbled into it, keeping his voice low but she could hear.

'Your husband has explained it was the day before,' his colleague said. 'And earlier – in his lunchtime – that his last visit to Miss Ritchie was.'

Katherine wanted to stay where she was now. She wanted to sleep, to be aware of the man she did not know well beside her, to have him waiting for her when she woke up. Because of the heatwave that had begun a week ago, he had turned the air-conditioning on, an old-fashioned contraption at the window.

'I have to go,' he said.

'Of course. I won't be long.'

Below them, another horse-race had come to its exciting stage, the commentary faintly reaching them as they dressed. They went together down uncarpeted, narrow stairs, past the open door of the betting shop.

'Shall you come again?' he asked.

'Yes.'

And they arranged an afternoon, ten days away because he could not always just walk out of the office where he worked.

'Don't let me talk about it,' she said before they parted. 'Don't ask, don't let me tell you.'

'If you don't want to.'

'It's all so done with. And it's a bore for you, or will be soon.'

He began to say it wasn't, that that was what the trouble was. She knew he began to say it because she could see it in his face before he changed his mind. And of course he was right; he wasn't a fool. Curiosity couldn't be just stifled.

They didn't embrace before he hurried off, for they had done all that. When she watched him go it felt like a habit already, and she wondered as she crossed the street to the Costa café if, with repetition, her afternoons here would acquire some variation of the order and patterns of the work she missed so. 'Oh, none at all,' she'd said when she'd been asked if there were prospects yet of something else. She had not said it was unlikely that again she'd make her morning journey across London, skilful in the overcrowded Tube stations, squeezing on to trains that were crowded also. Unlikely that there'd be, somewhere, her own small office again, her position of importance, and generous colleagues who made up for a bleakness and kept at bay its ghosts. She hadn't known until Phair said, not long ago, that routine, for him, often felt like an antidote to dementia.

She should not have told so much this afternoon, Katherine said to herself, sitting where she had sat before. She had never, to anyone else, told anything at all, or talked about what had happened to people who knew. I am unsettled, she thought; and, outside, rain came suddenly, with distant thunder, ending the heat that had become excessive.

When she'd finished her coffee Katherine didn't leave the café because she didn't have an umbrella. There had been rain that night too. Rain came into it because the elderly woman in the flat across the landing had looked out when it was just beginning, the six o'clock news on the radio just beginning too. The woman had remembered that earlier she had passed the wide-open window half a flight down the communal stairway and gone immediately to close it before, yet again, the carpet was drenched. It was while she was doing so that she heard the downstairs hall door opening and footsteps beginning on the stairs. When she reached her own door the man had reached the landing. 'No, I never thought anything untoward,' she had later stated apparently. Not anything untoward about the girl who occupied the flat across the landing, about the men who came visiting her. 'I didn't pry,' she said. She had turned round when she'd opened her front door and had caught a glimpse of the man who'd come that night. She'd seen him before, the way he stood waiting for the girl to let him in, his clothes, his hair, even his footfall on the stairs: there was no doubt at all.

The café filled up, the doorway crowded with people sheltering, others queuing at the counter. Katherine heard the staccato summons of her mobile phone, a sound she hated, although originally she'd chosen it herself. A voice that might have been a child's said something she couldn't understand and repeated it when she explained that she couldn't, and then the line went dead. So many voices were like a child's these days, she thought, returning the phone to her handbag. 'A fashion, that baby telephone voice,' Phair had said. 'Odd as it might seem.'

She nibbled the edge of her florentine, then opened the spill of sugar. The light outside had darkened and now was brightening again. The people in the doorway began to move away. It had rained all night the other time.

'Nothing again?' Phair always enquired when he came in. He was concerned about what had been so arbitrarily and unexpectedly imposed upon her, had once or twice brought back hearsay of vacancies. But even at his most solicitous, and his gentlest, he had himself to think about. It was worse for Phair and always would be, that stood to reason.

Her mobile telephone rang again and his voice said that in his lunch hour he'd bought asparagus because he'd noticed it on a stall, looking good and not expensive. They'd mentioned asparagus yesterday, realizing it was the season: she would have bought some if he hadn't rung. 'On the way out of the cinema,' she said, having already said that she'd just seen *La Strada* again. He'd tried for her an hour ago, he said, but her phone had been switched off. 'Well, yes, of course,' he said.

\*

Six months was the length of an affair that took place because something else was wrong: knowing more about all this than Katherine did, the man she met in the afternoons said that. And, as if he had always been aware that he would, when a little longer than six months had passed he returned to his wife. Since then, he had retained the room while this reunion settled – or perhaps in case it didn't – but his belongings were no longer there. The room looked bigger, yet dingier, without them.

'Why do you love your husband, Katherine? After all this – what he has put you through?'

'No one can answer that.'

'You hide from one another, you and he.'

'Yes.'

'Are you afraid, Katherine?'

'Yes. Both of us are afraid. We dream of her, we see her dead. And we know in the morning if the other one has. We know and do not say.'

'You shouldn't be afraid.'

They did not ever argue in the room, not even mildly, but disagreed and left it there. Or failed to understand and left that too. Katherine did not ask if a marriage could be shored up while this room was still theirs for a purpose. Her casual lover did not press her to reveal what she still withheld.

'I can't imagine him,' he said, but Katherine did not attempt to describe her husband, only commented that his first name suited him. A family name, she said.

'You're fairly remarkable, you know. To love so deeply.'

'And yet I'm here.'

'Perhaps I mean that.'

'More often than not, people don't know why they do things.'

'I envy you your seriousness. It's that I'd love you for.'

Once, when again he had to go, she stayed behind. He

was in a hurry that day; she wasn't quite ready. 'Just bang the door,' he said.

She listened to his footsteps clattering on the boards of the stairs and was reminded of the old woman saying she had recognized Phair's. Phair's lawyer would have asked in court if she was certain about that and would have wondered how she could be, since to have heard them on previous occasions she would each time have had to be on the landing, which surely was unlikely. He would have suggested that she appeared to spend more time on the communal landing than in her flat. He would have wondered that a passing stranger had left behind so clear an impression of his features, since any encounter there had been would have lasted hardly more than an instant.

Alone in the room, not wanting to leave it yet, Katherine crept back into the bed she'd left only minutes ago. She pulled the bedclothes up although it wasn't cold. The window curtains hadn't been drawn back and she was glad they hadn't. 'I didn't much care for that girl,' Phair said when the two policemen had gone. 'But I was fond of her in a different kind of way. I have to say that, Katherine. I'm sorry.' He had brought her coffee and made her sit there, where she was. Some men were like that, he said. 'We only talked. She told me things.' A girl like that took chances every time she answered her doorbell, he said; and when he cried Katherine knew it was for the girl, not for himself.

'Oh yes, I understand,' she said. 'Of course I do.' A sleazy relationship with a classy tart was what she understood, as he had understood when she told him she could not have children, when he'd said it didn't matter, although she knew it did.

'I've risked what was precious,' he whispered in his shame, and then confessed that deceiving her had been an excitement too. Risk came into it in all sorts of ways; risk was part of it, the secrecy of concealment, stealth. And risk had claimed its due.

The same policemen came back later. 'You're sure about that detail, madam?' they asked and afterwards, countless times, asked her that again, repeating the date and hearing her repeat that ten to seven was the usual time. Phair hadn't wanted to know – and didn't still – why she had answered as she had, why she continued to confirm that he'd returned ninety minutes sooner than he had. She couldn't have told him why, except to say that instinct answered for her, as bewilderment and confusion had when first she'd heard the question. She might have said she knew Phair as intimately as she knew herself, that it was impossible to imagine his taking the life of a girl no matter what his relationship with her had been. There was – she would have said if she'd been asked – the pain of that, of their being together, he and the girl, even if only for conversation. 'You quarrelled, sir?' the tall policeman enquired. You could see there'd been a quarrel, he insisted, no way you could say there hadn't been a disagreement that got out of hand. But Phair was not the quarrelling sort. He shook his head. In all his answers, he hadn't disputed much except responsibility for the death, had not denied he'd been a visitor to the flat, gave details as he remembered them. He accepted that his fingerprints were there, while they accepted nothing. 'You're sure, madam?' they asked again, and her instinct hardened, touched with apprehension, even though their implications were ridiculous. Yes, she was sure, she said. They said their spiel and then arrested him.

Katherine slept and when she woke did not know where she was. But only minutes had passed, fewer than ten. She washed at the basin in the corner, and slowly dressed. When he was taken from her, in custody until the trial's outcome, it was suggested at the Institute that they could manage without her for a while. 'No, no,' she had insisted. 'I would rather come.' And in the hiatus that followed – long and silent – she had not known that doubt began to spread in the frail memory of the elderly woman who in time would be called upon to testify to her statements on oath. She had not known that beneath the weight of importance the old woman was no longer certain that the man she'd seen on that wet evening – already shadowy – was a man she'd seen before. With coaching and encouragement, she would regain her confidence, it must have been believed by those for whom her evidence was essential: the prosecution case rested on this identification, on little else. But the long delay had taken a toll, the witness had been wearied by preparation, and did not, in court, conceal her worries. When the first morning of the trial was about to end, the judge calmed his anger to declare that in his opinion there was no case to answer. In the afternoon the jury was dismissed.

Katherine pulled back the curtains, settled her make-up, made the bed. Blame was there somewhere – in faulty recollection, in the carelessness of policemen, in a prosecution's ill-founded confidence – yet its attribution was hardly a source of satisfaction. Chance and circumstance had brought about a nightmare, and left it to a judge's invective to make a nonsense of it. He did so, but words were not enough: too much was left behind. No other man was ever charged, although of course there was another man.

She banged the door behind her, as she'd been told to. They had not said goodbye, yet as she went downstairs, hearing again the muffled gabble of the racecourse commentator, she knew it was for the last time. The room was finished with. This afternoon she had felt that, even if it had not been said.

She did not have coffee and walked by the Prince and Dog without noticing it. In her kitchen she would cook the food she'd bought and they would sit together and talk about the day. She would look across the table at the husband she loved and see a shadow there. They would speak of little things.

She wandered, going nowhere, leaving the bustling street that was gracious also, walking by terraced houses, lace-curtained windows. Her afternoon lover would mend the marriage that had failed, would piece by piece repair the damage because damage was not destruction and was not meant to be. To quarrel often was not too terrible; nor, without love, to be unfaithful. They would agree that they were up to this, and friendly time would do the rest, not asked to do too much. 'And she?' his wife one day might wonder, and he would say his other woman was a footnote to what had happened in their marriage. Perhaps that, no more.

Katherine came to the canal, where there were seats along the water. This evening she would lie, and they would speak again of little things. She would not say she was afraid, and nor would he. But fear was there, for her the nag of doubt, infecting him in ways she did not know about. She walked on past the seats, past children with a nurse. A barge with barrels went by, painted roses on its prow.

A wasteland, it seemed like where she walked, made so not by itself but by her mood. She felt an anonymity, a solitude here where she did not belong, and something came with that which she could not identify. Oh, but it's over, she told herself, as if in answer to this mild bewilderment, bewildering herself further and asking herself how she knew what she seemed to know. Thought was no good: all this was feeling. So, walking on, she did not think.

She sensed, without a reason, the dispersal of restraint. And yes, of course, for all nine years there'd been restraint. There'd been no asking to be told, no asking for promises that the truth was what she heard. There'd been no asking about the girl, how she'd dressed, her voice, her face, and if she only sat there talking, no more than that. There'd been no asking if there had really been the usual misery on the Northern line, the waiting for a taxi in the rain. For all nine years, while work for both of them allowed restraint, there had been silence in their ordinary exchanges, in conversation, in making love, in weekend walks and summer trips abroad. For all nine years love had been there, and more than just a comforter, too intense for that. Was stealth an excitement still? That was not asked and Katherine, pausing to watch another barge approaching, knew it never would be now. The flat was entered and Sharon Ritchie lay suffocated on her sofa. Had she been the victim kind? That, too, was locked away.

Katherine turned to walk back the way she'd come. It wouldn't be a shock, or even a surprise. He expected no more of her than what she'd given him, and she would choose her moment to say that she must go. He would understand; she would not have to tell him. The best that love could do was not enough, and he would know that also.

# Men of Ireland

The man came jauntily, the first of the foot passengers. Involuntarily he sniffed the air. My God! he said, not saying it aloud. My God, you can smell it all right. He hadn't been in Ireland for twenty-three years.

He went more cautiously when he reached the edge of the dock, being the first, not knowing where to go. 'On there,' an official looking after things said, gesturing over his shoulder with a raised thumb.

'OK,' the man said. 'OK.'

He went in this direction. The dock was different, not as he remembered it, and he wondered where the train came in. Not that he intended to take it, but it would give him his bearings. He could have asked the passengers who had come off the boat behind him but he was shy about that. He went more slowly and they began to pass him, some of them going in the same direction. Then he saw the train coming in. Dusty, it looked; beaten-up a bit, but as much of it as he could see was free of graffiti.

He was a shabbily dressed man, almost everything he wore having been abandoned by someone else. He had acquired the garments over a period, knowing he intended to make this journey – the trousers of what had been a suit, brown pin-striped, worn shiny in the seat and at the knees, a jacket that had been navy-blue and was nondescript now, the khaki shirt he wore an item once of military attire. His shoes were good; in one of his pockets was an Old Carthusian tie, although he had not himself attended Charterhouse. His name was Donal Prunty. Once big, heavily made, he seemed much less so now, the features of a face that had been florid at that time pinched within the sag of flesh. His dark hair was roughly cut. He was fifty-two years old.

The cars were coming off the boat now, beginning to wind their way around the new concrete buildings before passing through one of them – or so it seemed from where he stood. The road they were making for was what he wanted and he walked in that direction. Going over, the livestock lorry he'd been given a lift in had brought him nearly to the boat itself. Twenty-three years, he thought again, you'd never believe it.

He'd been on the road for seven days, across the breadth of England, through Wales. The clothes had held up well; he'd kept himself shaven as best he could, the blades saved up from what they allowed you in the hostels. You could use a blade thirty or so times if you wanted to, until it got jagged. You'd have to watch whatever you'd acquired for the feet; most of all you had to keep an eye on that department. His shoes were the pair he'd taken off the drunk who'd been lying on the street behind the Cavendish Hotel. Everything else you could take was gone from him – wallet, watch, studs and cufflinks, any loose change, a fountain pen if there'd been one, car keys in case the car would be around with things left in it. The tie had been taken off but thrown back and he had acquired it after he'd unlaced the shoes.

When he reached the road to Wexford the cars were on it already. Every minute or so another one would go past and the lorries were there, in more of a hurry. But neither car nor lorry stopped for him and he walked for a mile and then the greater part of another. Fewer passed him then, more travelling in the other direction, to catch the same boat going back to Fishguard. He caught up with a van parked in a lay-by, the driver eating crisps, a can of Pepsi-Cola on the dashboard in front of him, the window beside him wound down.

'Would you have a lift?' he asked him.

'Where're you heading?'

'Mullinavat.'

'I'm taking a rest.'

'I'm not in a hurry. God knows, I'm not.'

'I'd leave you to New Ross. Wait there till I'll have finished the grub.'

'D'you know beyond Mullinavat, over the Galloping Pass? A village by the name of Gleban?'

'I never heard of that.'

'There's a big white church out the road, nothing only petrol and a half-and-half in Gleban. A priests' seminary a half-mile the other way.'

'I don't know that place at all.'

'I used be there one time. I don't know would it be bigger now.'

'It would surely. Isn't everywhere these times? Get in and we'll make it to Ross.'

Prunty considered if he'd ask the van driver for money. He could leave it until they were getting near Ross in case the van would be pulled up as soon as money was mentioned and he'd be told to get out. Or maybe it'd be better if he'd leave it until the van was drawn up at the turn to Mullinavat, where there'd be the parting of the ways. He remembered Ross, he remembered where the Mullinavat road was. What harm could it do, when he was as far as he could be taken, that he'd ask for the price of a slice of bread, the way any traveller would?

Prunty thought about that while the van driver told him his mother was in care in Tagoat. He went to Tagoat on a Sunday, he said, and Prunty knew what the day was then, not that it made a difference. In a city you'd always know that one day of the week when it came round, but travelling you wouldn't be bothered cluttering yourself with that type of thing.

'She's with a woman who's on the level with her,' the van driver said. 'Not a home, nothing like that. I wouldn't touch a home.'

Prunty agreed that he was right. She'd been where she was a twelve-month, the van driver said, undisturbed in a room, every meal cooked while she'd wait for it. He wagged his head in wonder at these conditions. 'The Queen of Sheba,' he said.

Prunty's own mother was dead. She'd died eighteen months before he'd gone into exile, a day he hated remembering. Word came in at Cahill's, nineteen seventy-nine, a wet winter day, February he thought it was.

'You've only the one mother,' he said. 'I'm over for the same.'

Prunty made the connection in the hope that such shared ground would assist in the matter of touching the van driver for a few coins.

'In England, are you?' the van driver enquired.

'Oh, I am. A long time there.'

'I was never there yet.'

'I'm after coming off the ferry.'

'You're travelling light.'

'I have other stuff at Gleban.'

'Is your mother in a home there?'

'I wouldn't touch one, like yourself. She's eighty-three years of age, and still abiding in the same house eight children was born in. Not a speck of dust in it, not an egg fried you wouldn't offer up thanks for, two kinds of soda bread made every day.'

The van driver said he got the picture. They passed the turn to Adamstown, the evening still fine, which Prunty was glad about. He had two children, the van driver said, who'd be able to tell him if Kilkenny won. Going down to Tagoat on a Sunday was the way of it when old age would be in charge, he said; you made the sacrifice. He crossed himself when they passed a church, and Prunty said to himself he'd nearly forgotten that.

'You'd go through Wexford itself in the old days,' he said.

'You would all right.'

'The country's doing well.'

'The Europeans give us the roads. Ah, but sure she's doing well all the same.'

'Were you always in Ross?'

'Oh, I was.'

'I cleared off when I had to. A while back.'

'A lot went then.'

Prunty said you'd never have believed it at the time. It would be happening all around you and you wouldn't know the scale of the emigration. He was listened to without much interest. The conversation flagged and the van drew up when there'd been silence for a few miles. They were in a quiet street, deserted on a Sunday evening. Prunty was reluctant to get out.

'You couldn't see your way to a few bob?'

The van driver leaned across to release the catch of the door. He pushed the door open.

'Maybe a fifty if you'd have it handy,' Prunty suggested, and the van driver said he never carried money with him in the van and Prunty knew it wasn't true. He shook his head. He said: 'Any loose change at all.'

'I have to be getting on now. Take that left by the lamppost with the bin on it. D'you see it? Take it and keep going.'

Prunty got out. He stood back while the door was banged shut from the inside. They said it because the mention of money made them think of being robbed. Even a young fellow like that, strong as a horse. Hold on to what you'd have: they were all like that.

He watched the van driving away, the orange indicator light flicking on and off, the turn made to the right. He set off in the direction he'd been given and no car passed him until he left the town behind. None stopped for him then, the evening sun dazzling him on the open road. That was the first time he had begged in Ireland, he said to himself, and the thought stayed with him for a few miles, until he lay down at the edge of a field. The night would be fine except for the bit of dew that might come later on. It wasn't difficult to tell.

\*

The old man was asleep, head slumped into his chest, its white hair mussed, one arm hanging loose. The doorbell hadn't roused him, and Miss Brehany's decision was that she had no option but to wake him since she had knocked twice and still he hadn't heard. 'Father Meade,' she called softly, while the man who had come waited in the hall. She should have sent him away; she should have said come some time Father Meade would know to expect him; after his lunch when the day was warm he usually dropped off. 'Miss Brehany,' he said, sitting up.

She described the man who had come to the door. She said she had asked for a name but that her enquiry had been passed by as if it hadn't been heard. When she'd asked again she hadn't understood the response. She watched the priest pushing himself to his feet, the palms of his hands pressed hard on the surface of his desk.

'He's wearing a collar and tie,' she said.

'Would that be Johnny Healy?'

'It isn't, Father. It's a younger man than Johnny Healy.'

'Bring him in, Rose, bring him in. And bring me in a glass of water, would you?'

'I would of course.'

Father Meade didn't recognize the man who was brought to him, although he had known him once. He wasn't of the parish, he said to himself, unless he'd come into it in recent years. But his housekeeper was right about the collar and tie, an addition to a man's attire that in Father Meade's long experience of such matters placed a man. The rest of his clothing, Rose Brehany might have added, wasn't up to much.

'Would you remember me, Father? Would you remember Donal Prunty?'

Miss Brehany came in with the water and heard that asked and observed Father Meade's slow nod, after a pause. She was thanked for the glass of water.

'Are you Donal Prunty?' Father Meade asked.

'I served at the Mass for you, Father.'

'You did, Donal, you did.'

'It wasn't yourself who buried my mother.'

'Father Loughlin if it wasn't myself. You went away, Donal.'

'I did, all right. I was never back till now.'

He was begging. Father Meade knew, you always could tell; it was one of the senses that developed in a priest. Not that a lot came begging in a scattered parish, not like you'd get in the towns.

'Will we take a stroll in the garden, Donal?'

'Whatever would be right for you, Father. Whatever.'

Father Meade unlatched the french windows and went

ahead of his visitor. 'I'm fond of the garden,' he said, not turning his head.

'I'm on the streets, Father.'

'In Dublin, is it?'

'I went over to England, Father.'

'I think I maybe heard.'

'What work was there here, all the same?'

'Oh, I know, I know. Nineteen-what would it have been?'

'Nineteen eighty-one I went across.'

'You had no luck there?'

'I never had luck, Father.'

The old man walked slowly, the arthritis he was afflicted with in the small bones of both his feet a nuisance today. The house in which he had lived since he'd left the presbytery was modest, but the garden was large, looked after by a man the parish paid for. House and garden were parish property, kept for purposes such as this, where old priests – more than one at the same time if that happened to be how things were – would have a home. Father Meade was fortunate in having it to himself, Miss Brehany coming every day.

'Isn't it grand, that creeper?' He gestured across a strip of recently cut grass at Virginia creeper turning red on a high stone wall with broken glass in the cement at the top. Prunty had got into trouble. The recollection was vague at first, before more of it came back: stealing from farms at harvest time or the potato planting, when everyone would be in the fields. Always the same, except the time he was caught with the cancer box. As soon as his mother was buried he went off, and was in trouble again before he left the district a year or so later.

'The Michaelmas daisy is a flower that's a favourite of mine.' Father Meade gestured again. 'The way it cheers up the autumn.'

'I know what you mean all right, Father.'

They walked in silence for a few minutes. Then Father Meade asked: 'Are you back home to stop, Donal?'

'I don't know am I. Is there much doing in Gleban?'

'Ah, there is, there is. Well, look at it now, compared with when you took off. Sure, it's a metropolis nearly.' Father Meade laughed, then more seriously added: 'We've the John Deere agency, and the estate on the Mullinavat road and another beyond the church. We have the Super-Valu and the Hardware Co-op and the bank sub-office two days in the week. We have Dolan's garage and Linehan's drapery and general goods, and changes made in Steacy's. You'd go to Mullinavat for a doctor in the old days, even if you'd get one there. We have a young fellow coming out to us on a Tuesday for the last year and longer.'

A couple of steps, contending with the slope of the garden, broke the path they were on. The chair Father Meade had rested on to catch the morning sun was still there, on a lawn more spacious than the strip of grass by the wall with the Virginia creeper.

'Still and all, it's a good thing to come back to a place when you were born in it. I remember your mother.'

'I'm wondering could you spare me something, Father.'

Father Meade turned and began the walk back to the house. He nodded an indication that he had heard and noted the request, the impression given to Prunty that he was considering it. But in the room where he had earlier fallen asleep he said there was employment to be had in Gleban and its neighbourhood.

'When you'll go down past Steacy's bar go into Kingston's yard and tell Mr Kingston I sent you. If Mr Kingston hasn't something himself he'll put you right for somewhere else.'

'What's Kingston's yard?'

'It's where they bottle the water from the springs up at the Pass.'

'It wasn't work I came for, Father.'

★

Prunty sat down. He took out a packet of cigarettes, and then stood up again to offer it to the priest. Father Meade was standing by the french windows. He came further into the room and stood behind his desk, not wanting to sit down himself because it might be taken as an encouragement by his visitor to prolong his stay. He waved the cigarettes away.

'I wouldn't want to say it,' Prunty said.

He was experiencing difficulty with his cigarette, failing to light it although he struck two matches, and Father Meade wondered if there was something the matter with his hands the way he couldn't keep them steady. But Prunty said the matches were damp. You spent a night sleeping out and you got damp all over even though it didn't rain on you.

'What is it you don't want to say, Mr Prunty?'

Prunty laughed. His teeth were discoloured, almost black. 'Why're you calling me Mr Prunty, Father?'

The priest managed a laugh too. Put it down to age, he said: he sometimes forgot a name and then it would come back.

'Donal it is,' Prunty said.

'Of course it is. What's it you want to say, Donal?'

A match flared, and at once there was a smell of tobacco smoke in a room where no one smoked any more.

'Things happened the time I was a server, Father.'

'It was a little later on you went astray, Donal.'

'Have you a drink, Father? Would you offer me a drink?'

'We'll get Rose to bring us in a cup of tea.'

Prunty shook his head, a slight motion, hardly a movement at all.

'I don't keep strong drink,' Father Meade said. 'I don't take it myself.'

'You used give me a drink.'

'Ah no, no. What's it you want, Donal?'

'I'd estimate it was money, Father. If there's a man left anywhere would see me right it's the Father. I used say that. We'd be down under the arches and you could hear the rain falling on the river. We'd have the brazier going until they'd come and quench it. All Ireland'd be there, Toomey'd say. Men from all over, and Nellie Bonzer, too, and Colleen from Tuam. The methylated doing the rounds and your fingers would be shivering and you opening up the butts, and you'd hear the old stories then. Many's the time I'd tell them how you'd hold your hand up when you were above in the pulpit. 'Don't go till I'll give it to you in Irish,' you'd say, and you'd begin again and the women would sit there obedient, not understanding a word but it wouldn't matter because they'd have heard it already in the foreign tongue. Wasn't there many a priest called it the foreign tongue, Father?'

'I'm sorry you've fallen on hard times, Donal.'

'Eulala came over with a priest's infant inside her.'

'Donal –'

'Eulala has a leg taken off of her. She has the crutches the entire time, seventy-one years of age. It was long ago she left Ireland behind her.'

'Donal –'

'Don't mind me saying that about a priest.'

'It's a bad thing to say, Donal.'

'You used give me a drink. D'you remember that though? We'd sit down in the vestry when they'd all be gone. You'd look out the door to see was it all right and you'd close it and come over to me. "Isn't it your birthday?" you'd say, and it wouldn't be at all. "Will we open the old bottle?" you'd say. The time it was holy wine, you sat down beside me and said it wasn't holy yet. No harm, you said.'

Father Meade shook his head. He blinked, and frowned, and for a moment Miss Brehany seemed to be saying there was a man at the front door, her voice coming to him while he was still asleep. But he wasn't asleep, although he wanted to be.

'Many's the time there'd be giving out about the priests,' Prunty said. 'The hidden Ireland is Toomey's word for the way it was in the old days. All that, Father. "Close your eyes," you used say in the vestry. "Close your eyes, boy. Make your confession to me after."'

There was a silence in the room. Then Father Meade asked why he was being told lies, since he of all people would know they were lies. 'I think you should go away now,' he said.

'When I told my mother she said she'd have a whip taken to me.'

'You told your mother nothing. There was nothing to tell anyone.'

'Breda Flynn's who Eulala was, only a Romanian man called her that and she took it on. Limerick she came from. She was going with the Romanian. Toomey's a Carlow man.'

'What you're implying is sickening and terrible and disgraceful. I'm telling you to go now.'

Father Meade knew he said that, but hardly heard it because he was wondering if he was being confused with another priest: a brain addled by recourse to methylated spirits would naturally be blurred by now. But the priests of the parish, going back for longer than the span of Prunty's lifetime, had been well known to Father Meade. Not one of them could he consider, even for a moment, in the role Prunty was hinting at. Not a word of what was coming out of this demented imagination had ever been heard in the parish, no finger ever pointed in the direction of any priest. He'd have known, he'd have been told: of that Father Meade was certain, as sure of it as he was of his faith. 'I have no money for you, Prunty.'

'Long ago I'd see the young priests from the seminary. Maybe there'd be three of them walking together, out on the road to the Pass. They'd always be talking and I'd hear them and think maybe I'd enter the seminary myself. But then again you'd be cooped up. Would I come back tomorrow morning after you'd have a chance to get hold of a few shillings?'

'I have no money for you,' Father Meade said again.

'There's talk no man would want to put about. You'd forget things, Father. Long ago things would happen and you'd forget them. Sure, no one's blaming you for that. Only one night I said to myself I'll go back to Gleban.'

'Do you know you're telling lies, Prunty? Are you aware of it? Evil's never forgotten, Prunty: of all people, a priest knows that. Little things fall away from an old man's mind but what you're trying to put into it would never have left it.'

'No harm's meant, Father.'

'Tell your tale in Steacy's bar, Prunty, and maybe you'll be believed.'

Father Meade stood up and took what coins there were from his trouser pockets and made a handful of them on the desk.

'Make your confession, Prunty. Do that at least.'

\*

Prunty stared at the money, counting it with his eyes. Then he scooped it up. 'If we had a few notes to go with it,' he said, 'we'd have the sum done right.'

He spoke slowly, as if unhurried enunciation was easier for the elderly. It was all the talk, he said, the big money there'd be. No way you could miss the talk, no way it wouldn't affect you.

He knew he'd get more. Whatever was in the house he'd go away with, and he watched while a drawer was unlocked and opened, while money was taken from a cardboard box. None was left behind.

'Thanks, Father,' he said before he went.

\*

Father Meade opened the french windows in the hope that the cigarette smoke would blow away. He'd been a smoker himself, a thirty-a-day man, but that was long ago.

'I'm off now, Father,' Miss Brehany said, coming in to say it, before she went home. She had cut cold meat for him, she said. She'd put the tea things out for him, beside the kettle.

'Thanks, Rose. Thanks.'

She said goodbye and he put the chain on the hall door. In the garden he pulled the chair he'd been sitting on earlier into the last of the sun, and felt it warm on his face. He didn't blame himself for being angry, for becoming upset because he'd been repelled by what was said to him. He didn't blame Donal Prunty because you couldn't blame a hopeless case. In a long life a priest had many visits, heard voices that ages ago he'd forgotten, failed to recognize faces that had been as familiar as his own. 'See can you reach him, Father,' Donal Prunty's mother had pleaded when her son was still a child, and he had tried to. But Prunty had lied to him then too, promising without meaning it that he'd reform himself. 'Ah sure, I needed a bit of money,' he said hardly a week later when he was caught with the cancer box broken open.

Was it because he clearly still needed it, Father Meade wondered, that he'd let him go away with every penny in the house? Was it because you couldn't but pity him? Or was there a desperation in the giving, as if it had been prompted by his own failure when he'd been asked, in greater desperation, to reach a boy who didn't know right from wrong?

While he rested in the sun, Father Meade was aware of a temptation to let his reflections settle for one of these conclusions. But he knew, even without further thought, that there was as little truth in them as there was in the crude pretences of his visitor: there'd been no generous intent in the giving of the money, no honourable guilt had inspired the gesture, no charitable motive. He had paid for silence.

Guiltless, he was guilty, his brave defiance as much of a subterfuge as any of his visitor's. He might have belittled the petty offence that had occurred, so slight it was when you put it beside the betrayal of a Church and the shaming of Ireland's priesthood. He might have managed to say something decent to a Gleban man who was down and out in case it would bring consolation to the man, in case it would calm his conscience if maybe one day his conscience would nag. Instead he had been fearful, diminished by the sins that so deeply stained his cloth, distrustful of his people.

Father Meade remained in his garden until the shadows that had lengthened on his grass and his flower-beds were no longer there. The air turned cold. But he sat a little longer before he went back to the house to seek redemption, and to pray for Donal Prunty.

\*

Prunty walked through the town Gleban had become since he had lived in it. He didn't go to the church to make his confession, as he'd been advised. He didn't go into Steacy's bar, but passed both by, finding the way he had come in the early morning. He experienced no emotion, nor did it matter how the money had become his, only that it had. A single faint thought was that the town he left behind was again the place of his disgrace. He didn't care. He hadn't liked being in the town, he hadn't liked asking where the priest lived, or going there. He hadn't liked walking in the garden or making his demand, or even knowing that he would receive what he had come for in spite of twice being told he wouldn't. He would drink a bit of the money away tonight and reach the ferry tomorrow. He wouldn't hurry after that. Whatever pace he went at, the streets where he belonged would still be there.

# Cheating at Canasta

It was a Sunday evening; but Sunday, Mallory remembered, had always been as any other day at Harry's Bar. In the upstairs restaurant the waiters hurried with their loaded plates, calling out to one another above the noisy chatter. Turbot, *scaloppa alla Milanese*, grilled chops, scrambled eggs with bacon or smoked salmon, peas or *spinaci al burro*, mash done in a particularly delicious way: all were specialities here, where the waiters' most remarkable skill was their changing of the tablecloths with a sleight of hand that was admired a hundred times a night, and even occasionally applauded. Downstairs, Americans and Italians stood three or four deep at the bar and no one heard much of what anyone else said.

Bulky without being corpulent, sunburnt, blue-eyed, with the look of a weary traveller, Mallory was an Englishman in the middle years of his life and was, tonight, alone. Four of those years had passed since he had last sat down to dinner with his wife in Harry's Bar. 'You promise me you'll go back for both of us,' Julia had pleaded when she knew she would not be returning to Venice herself, and he had promised; but more time than he'd intended had slipped by before he had done so. 'What was it called?' Julia had tried to remember, and he said Harry's Bar.

The kir he'd asked for came. He ordered turbot, a Caesar salad first. He pointed at a Gavi that had not been on the wine list before. '*Perfetto!*' the waiter approved.

There was a pretence that Julia could still play cards, and in a way she could. On his visits they would sit together on the sofa in the drawing-room of her confinement and challenge one another in another game of Canasta, which so often they had played on their travels or in the garden of the house they'd lived in since their marriage, where their children had been born. 'No matter what,' Julia had said, aware then of what was coming, 'let's always play cards.' And they did; for even with her memory gone, a little more of it each day – her children taken, her house, her flowerbeds, belongings, clothes – their games in the communal drawing-room were a reality her affliction still allowed. Not that there was order in their games, not that they were games at all; but still her face lit up when she found a joker or a two among her cards, was pleased that she could do what her visitor was doing, even though she couldn't quite, even though once in a while she didn't know who he was. He picked up from the floor the Kings and Jacks, the eights and tens her fumbling fingers dropped. He put them to one side, it didn't matter where. He cheated at Canasta and she won.

The promise Julia had exacted from her husband had been her last insistence. Perturbation had already begun, a fringe of the greyness that was to claim her so early in her life. Because, tonight, he was alone where so often she had been with him, Mallory recalled with piercing rawness that request and his assent to it. He had not hesitated but had agreed immediately, wishing she had asked for something else. Would it have mattered much, he wondered in the crowded restaurant, if he had not at last made this journey, the first of the many she had wanted him to make? In the depths of her darkening twilight, if there still were places they belonged in a childhood he had not known, among shadows that were hers, not his, not theirs. In all that was forgotten how could it matter if a whim, forgotten too, was put aside, as the playing cards that fell from her hand were?

A table for six was lively in a corner, glasses raised; a birthday celebration it appeared to be. A couple who hadn't booked, or had come too early, were sent away. A tall, thin woman looked about her, searching for someone who wasn't there. The last time, Mallory remembered, their table had been by the door.

He went through the contents of his wallet: the familiar cards, the list of the telephone numbers he always brought abroad, some unused tickets for the Paris Métro, scraps of paper with nothing on them, coloured slips unnecessarily retained. Its *carte bancaire* stapled to it, the bill of his hotel in Paris was folded twice and was as bulky as his tidy wad of euro currency notes. *Lisa* someone had scribbled on the back of a fifty. His wine came.

He had travelled today from Monterosso, from the coast towns of the Cinque Terre, where often in September they had walked the mountain paths. The journey in the heat had been uncomfortable. He should have broken it, she would have said – a night in Milan, or

Brescia to look again at the Foppas and the convent. Of course he should have arranged that, Mallory reflected, and felt foolish that he hadn't, and then foolish for being where he was, among people who were here for pleasure, or reasons more sensible than his. It was immediately a relief when a distraction came, his melancholy interrupted by a man's voice.

'Why are you crying?' an American somewhere asked.

This almost certainly came from the table closest to his own, but all Mallory could see when he slightly turned his head was a salt-cellar on the corner of a tablecloth. There was no response to the question that had been asked, or none that he heard, and the silence that gathered went on. He leaned back in his chair, as if wishing to glance more easily at a framed black-and-white photograph on the wall – a street scene dominated by a towering flat-iron block. From what this movement allowed, he established that the girl who had been asked why she was crying wasn't crying now. Nor was there a handkerchief clenched in the slender, fragile-seeming fingers on the tablecloth. A fork in her other hand played with the peas on her plate, pushing them about. She wasn't eating.

A dressed-up child too young even to be at the beginning of a marriage, but instinctively Mallory knew that she was already the wife of the man who sat across the table from her. A white band drew hair as smooth as ebony back from her forehead. Her dress, black too, was severe in the same way, unpatterned, its only decoration the loop of a necklace that matched the single pearl of each small earring. Her beauty startled Mallory – the delicacy of her features, her deep, unsmiling eyes – and he could tell that there was more of it, lost now in the empty gravity of her discontent.

'A better fellow than I am.' Her husband was ruddy, hair tidily brushed and parted, the knot of a red silk tie neither too small nor clumsily large in its crisp white collar, his linen suit uncreased. Laughing slightly when there was no response, either, to his statement about someone else being a better fellow, he added: 'I mean, the sort who gets up early.'

Mallory wondered if they were what he'd heard called Scott Fitzgerald people, and for a moment imagined he had wondered it aloud – as if, after all, Julia had again come to Venice with him. It was their stylishness, their deportment, the young wife's beauty, her silence going on, that suggested Scott Fitzgerald, a surface held in spite of an unhappiness. 'Oh but,' Julia said, 'he's careless of her feelings.'

'*Prego, signore.*' The arrival of Mallory's Caesar salad shattered this interference with the truth, more properly claiming his attention and causing him to abandon his pretence of an interest in something that wasn't there. It was a younger waiter who brought the salad, who might even be the boy – grown up a bit – whom Julia had called the *primo piatto* boy and had tried her Italian on. While Mallory heard himself wished *buon appetito*, while the oil and vinegar were placed more conveniently on the table, he considered that yes, there was a likeness, certainly of manner. It hadn't been understood by the boy at first when Julia asked him in Italian how long he'd been a waiter, but then he'd said he had begun at Harry's Bar only a few days ago and had been nowhere before. '*Subito, signore,*' he promised now when Mallory asked for pepper, and poured more wine before he went away.

'I didn't know Geoffrey got up early.' At the table that was out of sight her voice was soft, the quietness of its tone registering more clearly than what it conveyed. Her husband said he hadn't caught this. 'I didn't know he got up early,' she repeated.

'It's not important that he does. It doesn't matter what time the man gets up. I only said it to explain that he and I aren't in any way alike.'

'I know you're not like Geoffrey.'

'Why were you crying?'

Again there was no answer, no indistinct murmur, no lilt in which words were lost.

'You're tired.'

'Not really.'

'I keep not hearing what you're saying.'

'I said I wasn't tired.'

Mallory didn't believe she hadn't been heard: her husband was closer to her than he was and he'd heard the 'Not really' himself. The scratchy irritation nurtured malevolence unpredictably in both of them, making her not say why she had cried and causing him to lie. My God, Mallory thought, what they are wasting!

'No one's blaming you for being tired. No one can help being tired.'

She didn't take that up and there was silence while,

again, the surface held and Mallory finished his Caesar salad. He was the only diner on his own in the upstairs restaurant, where for a moment on his arrival he had been faintly disappointed not to be recognized. He had recognized, himself, the features of the waiter who had led him to his table; there had later been that familiarity about the younger one; nor could he help remembering, from four years ago, the easy warmth of the welcome that had suggested stirrings of recognition then. But he hadn't been a man on his own four years ago, and naturally it was difficult for restaurant waiters when they were presented with only part of what there'd been before. And perhaps he was a little more crumpled than before; and four years was a longer lapse of time than there ever was in the past.

'My sister married Geoffrey,' the girl at the table behind him was saying.

'Yes, she did. And all I'm trying to say –'

'I know what you're saying.'

'It's just I wonder if you do.'

'You're saying I thought it would be like Geoffrey and Ellen. That I was looking forward to what isn't there.'

'It's hard to understand why anyone married Geoffrey.'

Tonight it didn't matter what they said. Dreary Geoffrey, who rose early to read his emails or scrutinize his bank statements, who liked to lead an ordered life, was enough tonight to nourish their need to punish one another. That her sister's marriage wasn't much was something to throw into their exchanges, to comment on tonight because it hadn't, perhaps, been touched upon before. 'Now, we don't know one single bit of that,' Julia in her occasionally stern way might have said, and seemed to say it now. 'Talk to me instead.'

He smiled. And across the restaurant a woman in the jolly birthday party waved at him – as if she thought he'd smiled at her, or imagined she must know him and couldn't place him, or just felt sorry for him, alone like that in such convivial surroundings. He nodded, not letting his smile go, then looked away. For all her moments of sternness, how often on their travels had Julia speculated as wildly as he ever had himself about people they didn't know! Lovers embracing in the Fauchon tea-rooms, the Japanese at the Uffizi, Germans in the Lido sun, or café-table chatterers anywhere. And they'd been listened to themselves, that stood to reason – he taken for a country doctor, Julia had maintained, and she an almoner or something like it. English both of them, of course, for anyone could tell, their voices confirmed as upper class when there'd been curiosity as to that.

'*Va bene?*' the waiter who'd been the *primo piatto* boy enquired, lifting away the Caesar-salad plate. 'Was fine?'

'*Va bene. Va bene.*'

'*Grazie, signore.*'

San Giovanni in Bragora was where the Cima *Baptism* they liked was: elusive on the train that morning and ever since, the name of the church came back. Sometimes when you looked it seemed that Christ was still in the shallow water, but looking again it wasn't so: the almost naked figure stood on dry land at the water's edge. The church of the Frari had Bellini's triptych; the saints he'd painted when he was over eighty were in San Giovanni Crisostomo. How could it make a difference, not going again, alone, to admire them? Or standing or not standing before the Vivarini *Annunciation* in San Giobbe and whatever there was in Madonna dell'Orto? She'd be asleep now. As early as five o'clock they were put to bed sometimes.

'I'm not,' the girl was saying. 'If we're telling the truth, I'm not.'

'No one can expect to be happy all the time.'

'You asked me. I'm telling you because you asked me.'

Their waiter brought them raspberries, with meringue and ice-cream. Mallory watched the confections going by and heard the murmurs of the husband.

'Why have we ordered this?' the girl complained when the waiter had gone.

'You wanted it.'

'Why did you say I should have married Geoffrey?'

'I didn't say –'

'Well, whatever.'

'Darling, you're tired.'

'Why did we come here?'

'Someone told us it was good.'

'Why did we come to Venice?'

It was his turn not to reply. Marriage was an uncalculated risk, Mallory remembered saying once. The trickiest of all undertakings, he might have called it, might even have suggested that knowing this was an insurance against the worst, a necessary awareness of what unwelcome surprises there might be. 'At least that's something,' Julia had agreed, and said she hoped it was enough. 'Love's cruel angels at play,' she called it when they upset one another.

The quiet at the other table went on. '*Grazie mille, signore,*' Mallory heard when eventually it was broken, the bill paid then. He heard the chairs pulled back and then the couple who had quarrelled passed close to where he sat and on an impulse he looked up and spoke to them. He wondered as he did so if he had already had too much to drink, for it wasn't like him to importune strangers. He raised a hand in a gesture of farewell, hoping they would go on. But they hesitated, and he sensed their realization that he, who so clearly was not American, was English. There was a moment of disbelief, and then acceptance. This registered in their features, and shame crept in before the stylishness that had dissipated in the course of their quarrel returned to come to their rescue. His polite goodwill in wishing them good evening as they went by was politely acknowledged, smiles and pleasantness the harmless lies in their denial of all he'd heard. 'Its reputation's not exaggerated,' the husband commented with easy charm. 'It's good, this place.' Her chops had been delicious, she said.

Falling in with this, Mallory asked them if it was their first time in Venice. Embarrassment was still there, but they somehow managed to make it seem like their re-proval of themselves for inflicting their bickering on him.

'Oh, very much so,' they said together, each seeming instinctively to know how their answer should be given.

'Not yours, I guess?' the husband added, and Mallory shook his head. He'd been coming to Venice since first he'd been able to afford it, he said. And then he told them why he was here alone.

While he did so Mallory sensed in his voice an echo of his regret that foolishness had brought him here. He did not say it. He did not say that he was here to honour a whim that would have been forgotten as soon as it was expressed. He did not deplore a tiresome, futile journey. But he'd come close to doing so and felt ashamed in turn. His manner had dismissed the scratchiness he'd eavesdropped on as the unseemly stuff of marriage. It was more difficult to dismiss his own sly aberration, and shame still nagged.

'I'm sorry about your wife.' The girl's smile was gentle. 'I'm very sorry.'

'Ah, well.' Belittling melancholy, he shook his head.

Again the playing cards fall. Again he picks them up. She wins and then is happy, not knowing why.

The party at the corner table came to an end, its chatter louder, then subdued. A handbag left behind was rescued by a waiter. Other people came.

Tomorrow what has been lost in recollection's collapse will be restored as she has known it: the pink and gold of Sant Giobbe's *Annunciation*, its dove, its Virgin's features, its little trees, its God. Tomorrow the silenced music will play in the piazza of San Marco, and tourists shuffle in the *calles*, and the boats go out to the islands. Tomorrow the cats of Venice will be fed by ladies in the dried-out parks, and there'll be coffee on the Zattere.

'No, no,' he murmured when the husband said he was sorry too. 'No, no.'

He watched the couple go, and smiled across the crowded restaurant when they reached the door. Shame isn't bad, her voice from somewhere else insists. Nor the humility that is its gift.

# Bravado

The leaves had begun to fall. All along Sunderland Avenue on the pavement beneath the beech trees there was a sprinkling, not yet the mushy inconvenience they would become when more fell and rain came, which inevitably would be soon. Not many people were about; it was after midnight, almost one o'clock, the widely spaced lampposts casting pools of misty yellow illumination. A man walked his dog in Blenning Road in the same blotchy lamplight, the first of autumn's leaves gathering there also. An upstairs window opened in Verdun Crescent, hands clapped to dismiss a cat rooting in a flowerbed. A car turned into Sunderland Avenue, its headlights dimmed and then extinguished, its alarm set for the night with a flurry of flashing orange and red. The traffic of the city was a hum that only faintly reached these leisurely streets, the occasional distant shriek of a police siren or an ambulance more urgently disturbing their peace.

Less than half a mile away, the night was different. Young people prowled about outside the Star nightclub, its band – Big City – taking a break. A late shop was still open, a watchful Indian at the door noting who came and went. A few cars drew away, but more remained. Then, with a thump of such suddenness that for a moment it might have been taken as a warning of emergency or disaster, music again burst from the Star nightclub.

By half past one this neighbourhood, too, had quietened. The bouncers at the Star drove off, couples made their way to the dark seclusion of the nearby canal bank. Others stood about, groups forming and dispersing. Locking up his shop, the Indian was argued with, and abused when demands for alcohol and potato crisps were refused. The last of the parked cars were driven off.

Two youths who were friends went together, undaunted by the prospect of an hour's walk to where they lived. One was in shirtsleeves although it was chilly, the arms of a red anorak tied around his shoulders; the other wore a black woollen jersey above ragged jeans. They talked about the girls they had come across on the dancefloor, one in particular, well known to them both, the others strangers. They talked about their intentions for the future: in the Merchant Navy and in car sales, an uncle's business. These were the changes that were soon to come about, when education ended, when so much they had known for so long was to be left behind for ever: the Brothers and the lay teachers, the cramped desks scratched with entwined initials and hearts and arrows, all they had learned of self-preservation and of survival's cunning. There was, in their conversation, an absence of regret.

They paused in their walk while the anorak was unknotted and put on, zipped up and buttoned. Their evening out had been a good one, they agreed while this was being done. 'Kicking,' one said. 'Big City can do it.' They walked on, talking about that band's touch of genius.

With his mobile telephone close to his mouth, the Indian loudly demanded the police: his usual ploy at this hour, speaking to no one. His tormentors swore at him, then tired of their invective and went away. Five there were, two of them girls, neither of whom had taken part in the abuse of the Indian; which had surprised him, for girls were often the worst. He kept an eye on the five when they moved off in a bunch, causing an oncoming car to slow down to a crawl as they crossed the street. Then he locked his shop, thankful that there hadn't been an incident.

'Howya doin'?' Manning shouted at the driver of the car. He drummed on the bonnet with his fists and, joining in, his companions – but not the girls – did the same. The car kept moving, then stopped and reversed. It went another way.

'Could you beat that?' Manning laughed, watching the car from the middle of the road. He was tallest of the bunch, his reddish hair falling over his forehead in a floppy shock that he was said to be proud of. An air of insouciance distinguished his manner, was there again in the lazy saunter of his walk, in his smile. Manning led when he was with Donovan and Kilroy, which he was most of the time, and was tonight. Aisling was his girl, fair-haired and pretty, with expressive blue eyes, younger than Manning by more than a year. The second girl wasn't known to the others; earlier she had asked which way they were going and then asked if she could go with them because she lived in that direction. Francie she was called.

Aisling clung to Manning as they walked. With his arm round Francie, Kilroy tried to slow her down, in the hope of setting up an opportunity for something when they had fallen far enough behind. But Francie, aware of his intention, kept up a steady pace. She was small, often called a little thing, but deliberate and determined in her manner. She, too, was pretty, but less dramatically so than Aisling, whom Manning liked to describe as drop-dead gorgeous. She denied that she was, but Manning's regular repetition of the compliment did not displease her.

She listened to him now, saying he didn't intend to set foot in the Star again, objecting to the way the shaven-headed bouncers had frisked him for miniatures. They had taken one from him and afterwards said they hadn't: they thought they owned you, louts like that. 'Did you ever do a line, cowboy?' he called across Aisling to Donovan.

'Amn't I doing one with Emir Flynn?'

'You eejit!'

Laughing again, Manning sounded drunk. Not very, Aisling thought, but a little. She'd been drunk once or twice herself but hadn't liked it, everything slipping about, and the way you felt in the morning.

'Did you ever, though?' Manning pressed, offering Donovan a cigarette.

Donovan said he had of course, many a time, and Aisling knew all this was for her and for the girl who'd tagged along, whose name she had forgotten. 'Fanbloodytastic,' Donovan said, he and Manning lighting their cigarettes, sharing the match. No one else was a smoker.

They were going by the dyeworks now, where Manning had once climbed over the high spiked railings. That had been for Aisling too, and a girl called Maura Bannerman. The security lights had been triggered and through the railings they had watched Manning roaming about, from time to time peering in at the downstairs windows of the lumpy red-brick building that was said to have been a lunatic asylum once.

Behind her Aisling heard Kilroy telling the girl he had monopolized about that night. At the top of the railings, razor-wire was woven through the spikes, adding to the hazards: none of them knew how Manning had done it, but somehow he had, even though he was a bit drunk then too.

Kilroy had slit eyes that aptly suggested an untrustworthy nature. Donovan was considered to be dense: almost as tall as Manning, he was bulkier, clumsy in his movements, slow of speech. Kilroy had a stunted appearance, accentuated by oiled black hair sleekly brushed straight back, making the top of his head seem flat. Aisling didn't much like either of them.

The first time she'd been in the Star – the first time she'd seen Manning, no more than a face in the crowd – she had admired him. He'd noticed her interest, he told her afterwards; he said she was his kind, and she didn't hesitate when he asked her to go out with him. Mano he was called in the Dublin manner, Martin John his given names. Martin was what his family called him and Aisling thought of him as that when she was in her convent classroom, and every night before she went to sleep. She and he were an item, he said, which Aisling had never been with anyone before.

'I'd give a thousand bucks for a snort,' he was saying now, his voice slightly raised, a laugh in it again. 'Where'd we get ourselves a snort, cowboy?'

Donovan said maybe Dirty Doyle's, Kilroy suggested Capel Street. It was a kind of play; Martin Manning doing the big fellow, her father would have said. Aisling had become used to it ages ago.

They reached the quiet streets, St Stephen's Church at the corner of Goodchild Street, the shadowy sprawl of trees on either side of Sunderland Avenue ahead of them.

'Who're those geeks?' Donovan suddenly exclaimed and they all stopped, not knowing where to look at first. But when Francie pointed they saw the red anorak.

'It's bloody Dalgety,' Manning said.

*

The two parted in Sunderland Avenue, Dalgety turning into Blenning Road. On his own, he went a little faster, but paused when he noticed that one of the garden gates he was passing was invitingly open. He went through it and crossed a lawn to a corner near the house where he couldn't be seen from the windows. He urinated in the shadow of an eleagnus bush.

Once or twice, making their way from the nightclub, they had been aware of voices behind them but, engrossed in conversation themselves, they hadn't looked round to see whose they were. Dalgety couldn't hear the voices now and imagined that whoever they belonged to had gone in some other direction. A light hadn't come on in the house, which sometimes happened when you found a garden that was convenient for the purpose he had used it for. He unzipped his anorak because he'd noticed that the teeth of the zip hadn't been properly aligned. While he was zipping it up again he was struck, a blow on the right side of his head. He thought that someone had come out of the house, and was thinking he hadn't heard the front door opening when the next blow came. He stumbled and fell, and a foot smashed into his jaw when he was lying on the grass. He tried to stand up but couldn't.

*

Aisling had watched, not wanting to but she had. Francie had looked away when she saw what was happening. In the garden, standing back at first, not taking part, Donovan moved forward when the boy was lying on the grass. Kilroy stayed with the girl, calculating that he'd lose out with her if he joined in. Nobody spoke while the assault was taking place, not in the garden, not on the road. Nobody did when they all moved on, in a bunch again.

Aisling wondered what the boy had done, what insults had been exchanged in the Star or before that, how the boy had offended. Something of the headiness of the nightclub seemed to be there again, something of the music's energy, of the wildness that was often in a face as it went by on the dance-floor before it was sucked into the suffocating closeness of the crowd.

'Oh, leave me be!' Francie suddenly cried out. 'Just leave me, would you!'

'Behave yourself, cowboy.' Manning's rebuke came lightly, and for a moment Aisling saw the white gleam of his teeth.

Kilroy muttered, and desisted for a few minutes before he tried again and was again shaken off. In Charleston Road Francie parted from them, scuttling off, not saying goodnight. Kilroy hesitated, but didn't follow her.

'Dalgety's a tit,' Manning said when Aisling asked why Dalgety had been duffed up. 'Forget it,' he said.

'I never heard that name before,' Aisling said. 'Dalgety.'

'Yeah, a nerd's.'

Conversation lapsed then, but passing the entrance to the Greenbanks Hotel Donovan began on a story about his sister, how she was going to a shrink, and hated it so much she often didn't turn up for her weekly sessions.

'Some guy comes on heavy,' Donovan said. 'You end up with a shrink.'

Nobody commented. Donovan did not go on; the interrupted silence held. So that was it, Aisling thought, and felt relieved, aware of a relaxation in her body, as if her nerves had been strung up and no longer were. This Dalgety had upset Donovan's sister, going too far when she didn't want him to, whatever form his persistence took putting her in need of psychiatric care. And the anger Aisling had witnessed in the garden touched her, what had happened seeming different, less than it had been while she watched.

'See you, Mano,' Donovan said. 'Cheers, Aisling.'

She said goodnight. Donovan turned into Cambridge Road, and soon afterwards Kilroy turned off, too.

'All right, was he?' Aisling asked then.

'Who's this?'

'Dalgety.'

'Christ, of course he was.'

They went to Spire View Lane, where they always went when it was as late as this. 'You're a dazzler to-night,' Manning whispered, slipping his hands beneath her clothes.

She closed her eyes, kissing him back, his early-morning stubble harsh on her chin. The first time she had experienced that roughness it had excited her, and every time since it had. 'I'd best be getting back,' she said, not that she wanted to get back anywhere.

A dog came sniffing at them, some kind of small breed, black or grey, you couldn't tell in the dark. Someone whistled for it and it ran off.

'I'll walk you over,' Manning said, which he always did when she had to go. He lit a cigarette, as he always did too. The smoke would get into her clothes and she'd be asked about it if there was anyone still downstairs, although usually nobody was.

'I looked back,' Manning said. 'He was up on his feet.'

*

*Bernadette rang*, a note for her in the kitchen said, *and Sister Teresa about knowing your part for Thursday*.

No one was still up or there wouldn't be the note. Aisling made cocoa and had biscuits with it, sitting at the table with the *Evening Herald*, then pushing it away. She wished it hadn't happened, but thought about Hazel Donovan so badly affected that she had to be taken to a shrink and before she finished her cocoa she wondered if she really wished it. She might have stopped him but she hadn't, and she remembered now not wanting to. 'The hard man,' his friends said when they greeted him, knowing him well, knowing he took chances. 'Aw, come on,' he had urged, the time he gave her a lift on the bar of his bicycle, when they were caught by her father coming towards them on a bicycle too, his veterinary bag hanging on the handlebars. 'Don't ever let me see the like of that again,' her father stormed at her when she returned to the house. Being his favourite made being caught all the worse, her mother explained. Neither of them approved of Martin Manning. They didn't understand.

She washed the mug she'd drunk her cocoa from at the sink and put the lid on the biscuit tin. She picked up Sister Teresa's typed sheets and went upstairs. *Scenes from Hamlet* was Sister Teresa's title for the monologues she had put together, the first time she had attempted something that wasn't a conventional play. *That's fennel for you*, Aisling murmured, half asleep already, *and columbines . . .*

\*

At Number 6 Blenning Road the elderly woman who had lived alone there since she was widowed seven months ago was roused from a dream in which she was a child again. She went to the top of her stairs, leaned over the banister, and shouted in the direction of the hall door, asking who was there. But all that happened was the ringing of the doorbell again. It would take more than that, she told herself, to get her to open her door at this hour.

When the bell ceased there was a banging and a rapping, and a voice coming from far away because she hadn't had time to put her deaf-aids in. Even when the letterbox rattled and the voice was louder she still couldn't hear a word of what was said. She went back to her bedroom for her deaf-aids and then trudged down to the hall.

'What d'you want?' she shouted at the letterbox.

Fingers appeared, pressing the flap open.

'Excuse me, missus. Excuse me, but there's someone lying down in your garden.'

'It's half past six in the morning.'

'Could you phone up the guards, missus?'

In the hall she shook her head, not answering that. She asked whereabouts in her garden the person was.

'Just lying there on the grass. I'd call them up myself only my mobile's run out.'

She telephoned. No point in not, she thought. She was glad to be leaving this house, which for so long had been too big for two and was now ridiculously big for one. She had been glad before this, but now was more certain than ever that she had made the right decision. She thought so again while she watched from her dining-room window a Garda car arriving, and an ambulance soon after that. She opened her hall door then, and saw a body taken away. A man came to speak to her, saying it was he who had talked to her through the letterbox. A guard told her the person they had found lying near her eleagnus was dead.

★

On the news the address was not revealed. A front garden, it was reported, and gave the district. A milkman going by on his way to the depot had noticed. No more than that.

When Aisling came down at five past eight they were talking about it in the kitchen. She knew at once.

'You all right?' her mother asked, and she said she was. She went back to her bedroom, saying she had forgotten something.

★

It was all there on the front page of the *Evening Herald*'s early-afternoon edition. No charges had been laid, but it was expected that they would be later in the day. The deceased had not been known to the householder in whose garden the body had been discovered, who was reported as saying she had not been roused by anything unusual in the night. The identity of the deceased had not yet been established, but a few details were given, little more than that a boy of about sixteen had met his death following an assault. Witnesses were asked to come forward.

Aisling didn't; the girl who had tagged along did. The victim's companion on the walk from the Star night-club gave the time they left it, and the approximate time of their parting from one another. The nightclub bouncers were helpful but could add little to what was already known. The girl who had come forward was detained for several hours at the Garda station from which enquiries were being made. She was compli-mented on the clarity of her evidence and pressed to recall the names of the four people she had been with. But she had never known those names, only that the red-haired boy was called Mano and had himself addressed two of his companions as 'cowboy'. Arrests were made just before midnight.

Aisling read all that the next morning in the *Irish Independent*, which was the newspaper that came to the house. Later in the day she read an almost identical account in the *Irish Times*, which she bought in a news-agent's where she wasn't known. Both reports referred to her, describing her as 'the second girl', whom the gardaí were keen to locate. There was a photograph, a coat thrown over the head and shoulders of a figure being led away, a wrist handcuffed to that of a uniformed Garda. The second arrest, at a house in Ranelagh, told no more. No names were released at first.

When they were, Aisling made a statement, confessing

that she was the second girl, and in doing so she became part of what had happened. People didn't attempt to talk to her about it, and at the convent it was forbidden that they should do so; but it was sometimes difficult, even for strangers, to constrain the curiosity that too often was evident in their features. When more time passed there was the trial, and then the verdict: acquitted of murder, the two who had been apprehended were sent to gaol for eleven years, their previous good conduct taken into account, together with the consideration, undenied by the court, that there was an accidental element in what had befallen them: neither had known of their victim's frail, imperfect heart.

Aisling's father did not repeat his castigation of her for making a friendship he had never liked: what had happened was too terrible for petty blame. And her father, beneath an intolerant surface, could draw on gentleness, daily offering comfort to the animals he tended. 'We have to live with this,' he said, as if accepting that the violence of the incident reached out for him too, that guilt was indiscriminately scattered.

For Aisling, time passing was stranger than she had ever known days and nights to be before. Nothing was unaffected. In conveying the poetry of Shakespeare on the hastily assembled convent stage she perfectly knew her lines, and the audience was kind. But there was pity in that applause, because she had unfairly suffered in the aftermath of the tragedy she had witnessed. She knew there was, and in the depths of her consciousness it felt like mockery and she did not know why.

A letter came, long afterwards, flamboyant handwriting bringing back the excitement of surreptitious notes in the past. No claim was made on her, nor were there protestations of devotion, as once, so often, there had been. He would go away. He would bother no one. He was a different person now. A priest was being helpful.

The letter was long enough for contrition, but still was short. Missing from its single page was what had been missing, also, during the court hearing: that the victim had been a nuisance to Donovan's sister. In the newspaper photograph – the same one many times – Dalgety had been dark-haired, smiling only slightly, his features regular, almost nondescript except for a mole on his chin. And seeing it so often, Aisling had each time imagined his unwanted advances pressed on Hazel Donovan, and had read the innocence in those features as a lie. It was extraordinary that this, as the reason for the assault, had not been brought forward in the court; and more extraordinary that it wasn't touched upon in a letter where, with remorse and regret, it surely belonged. 'Some guy comes on heavy,' Donovan, that night, had said.

There had been a lingering silence and he broke it to mention this trouble in his family, as if he thought that someone should say something. The conversational tone of his voice seemed to indicate he would go on, but he didn't. Hungry for mercy, she too eagerly wove into his clumsy effort at distraction an identity he had not supplied, allowing it to be the truth, until time wore the deception out.

After the convent, Aisling acquired a qualification that led to a post in the general office of educational publishers. She had come to like being alone and often in the evenings went on her own to the cinema, and at weekends walked at Howth or by the sea at Dalkey. One afternoon she visited the grave, then went back often. A stone had been put there, its freshly incised words brief: the name, the dates. People came and went among the graves but did not come to this one, although flowers were left from time to time.

In a bleak cemetery Aisling begged forgiveness of the dead for the falsity she had embraced when what there was had been too ugly to accept. Silent, she had watched an act committed to impress her, to deserve her love, as other acts had been. And watching, there was pleasure. If only for a moment, but still there had been.

She might go away herself, and often thought she would: in the calm of another time and place to flee the shadows of bravado. Instead she stayed, a different person too, belonging where the thing had happened.

# An Afternoon

Jasmin knew he was going to be different, no way he couldn't be, no way he'd be wearing a baseball cap backwards over a number-one cut, or be gawky like Lukie Giggs, or make the clucking noise that Darren Finn made when he was trying to get a word out. She couldn't have guessed; all she knew was he wouldn't be like them. Could be he'd put you in mind of the Rawdeal drummer, whatever his name was, or of Al in *Doc Martin*. But the boy at the bus station wasn't like either. And he wasn't a boy, not for a minute.

He was the only person waiting who was alone apart from herself, and he didn't seem interested in the announcements about which buses were arriving or about to go. He didn't look up when people came in. He hadn't glanced once in her direction.

In the end, if nothing happened, Jasmin knew she would have to be brazen. She called it that to herself because it was what it amounted to, because you didn't get anywhere if you weren't. All your life you'd be carrying teas to the lorrymen in the diner, wiping down the tables and clearing away plastic plates, doing yourself an injury because you were soaking up the lorrymen's cigarette smoke. 'Now, you don't be brazen, Angie,' her mother used to scold her when she was no more than five or six and used to reach up for the cooking dates or a chocolate bar in Pricerite, opening whatever it was before her mother saw.

'You carry that to a woman doing the shelves. You say a mistake, you tell her that. Brazen you are,' her mother always ended up. 'You just watch it, girl.' She kept quiet herself. She never approached a woman who was arranging the shelves, just put whatever she'd taken behind the cornflakes or the kitchen rolls.

Jasmin was her own choice of name, since she'd always detested Angie and considered it common when she was older. 'Oh, la-di-da!' her mother's riposte had been to this further evidence of brazenness. 'Listen to our madam!' she would urge Holby, trying to draw the husband she had now into it, but Holby had become fly about things like that, having learned a lesson when he'd been drawn into a no-go marriage. It wasn't even the way you spelled it, her mother witheringly commented, no 'e' at the end was your bloody Muslim way. But when her mother wasn't there Holby said all that was a load of rubbish. 'You spell your name like it suits you,' he advised. 'You stick to how you want it.' Her mother was a violent woman, Jasmin considered, and knew that Holby did too.

'Excuse me,' she said, crossing to where the man was waiting. 'I'm Jasmin.'

He smiled at her. He had a peaky face, his teeth crowded at the front, light-coloured hair left long. He was wearing flannel trousers and a jacket, and that surprised her. A kind of speckled navy-blue the jacket was, with a grey tie. And shoes, not trainers, all very tidy. What surprised her more than anything was that he could have been mid-thirties, maybe a few years older. From his voice on the chat line, she'd thought more like nineteen.

'You fancy a coffee, Jasmin?' he said.

She felt excited when he spoke. The first time, on the chat line, she'd felt it when he'd called her Jasmin. Then again yesterday, when he'd said why don't they meet up?

'Yeah, sure,' she said.

All the time he kept his smile going. He was the happy sort, he'd told her on the chat line, not the first time, maybe the third or fourth. He'd asked her if she was the happy sort herself and she'd said yes, even though she knew she wasn't. Droopy was what she was, she'd heard her mother saying when Holby first came to live in the house; and later on, when her mother wasn't there, Holby asked her what the trouble was and she said nothing. 'Missing your dad?' Holby suggested. Seven she'd been then.

'You like to go in here?' the man suggested when they came to a McDonald's. 'You all right with a McDonald's, Jasmin?'

Just coffee, she said when he offered her a burger, and he said he'd bring it to her. Her father had gone when he found out her mother was going with Holby. Her mother said she didn't care, but six months later she made Holby marry her, because she'd been caught, she maintained, having not been married to Jasmin's father.

'I like a McDonald's,' the man said, coming with the coffee.

He was smiling again, and she wondered if he had smiled all the time at the counter. She didn't know his name. Three weeks ago she first heard his voice on the chat line. 'I'm Jasmin,' she'd said, expecting him to say his name also, but he hadn't.

'I could nearly tell your age,' he said now. 'From talking to you I nearly could.'

'Sixteen.'

'I thought sixteen.'

They sat at the counter that ran along the window. People on the pavement outside were in a hurry, jostling one another, no cars or buses allowed in this street.

'You're pretty,' he said. 'You're pretty, Jasmin.'

\*

She wasn't really. She couldn't be called pretty, but he said it anyway, and he wondered if there was a similar flattery he would particularly enjoy himself. While they watched the people on the street he thought about that, imagining the baby voice in which she gabbled her words saying something like he knew his way around, or saying he had an easy way with him.

'You think I'd be younger?' he asked her.

'Yeah, maybe.' She gave a little shrug, her thin shoulders jerking rapidly up and down. The blue anorak she wore wasn't grubby but had a faded, washed-out look. Other girls would have thrown it away.

'I like your charm,' he said, and pointed because she didn't know he meant the brooch that was pinned to the flimsy pink material of her dress. Her chest was flat and he could have said he liked that too because it was the truth. But the truth didn't always do, as he had long ago learned, and he smiled instead. Her bare, pale legs were like twigs stripped of their bark and he remembered how he used to do that, long ago too. Her shoes were pinkish, high-heeled.

'It's nothing,' she said, referring to her brooch. She shrugged in the same jerky way again, a spasm it seemed almost, although he knew it wasn't. 'A fish,' she said. 'It's meant to be a fish.'

'It's beautiful, Jasmin.'

'Holby gave it to me.'

'Who's Holby then?'

'My mother got married to him.'

'Your father, is this?'

'Bloody not.'

He smiled. In one of their conversations he'd asked her if she was pretty and she'd said maybe and he'd guessed she wasn't from the way she'd said it. They went in for fantasy, they put things on. Well, everyone did, of course.

'Same age as you, Jasmin – you think that when we talked? What age you think?'

'You didn't sound a kid,' she said.

She had a stud in one side of her nose and a little coil pierced into the edge of one ear. He wondered if she had something in her belly-button and wanted to ask her but knew not to. He wanted to close his eyes and think about a gleam of something nestling there, but he smiled instead. Her hair was lank, no frizziness left in it, brightened with a colouring.

'You take trouble,' he said. 'I thought you'd be the kind. I could tell you'd take trouble with yourself.'

Again there was the shrug. She held the paper coffee mug between her hands as if for warmth. She asked him if he was in work and he said yes, the law.

'The law? With the police?' She looked around, an agitated movement, her eyes alarmed. He could take her hand, he thought, a natural thing to do, but he resisted that too.

'The courts,' he said. 'If there's a dispute, if there's trouble I have to put a case. No, not the police, nothing to do with the police.'

She nodded, unease draining away.

'You going to be a nurse, Jasmin? Caring for people? I see you caring for people, Jasmin.'

When they asked, he always said the courts. And usually he said he could see them caring for people.

★

The Gold Mine was a place he knew and they went there to play the fruit machines. He always won, he said, but today he didn't. He didn't mind that. He didn't raise the roof like Giggs did when his money went for nothing. He didn't say the whole thing was fixed. Good days, bad days, was all he said.

'No, you take it,' he said when she had to explain she hadn't any money, and in the end she took the two-pound coin he gave to where they broke it down for her. He picked up a necklace for her with the grab, guiding the grab skilfully, knowing when to open the metal teeth and knowing not to be in a hurry to close them, to wait until he was certain. He'd cleared out everything there was on offer once, he said – sweets, jewellery, dice, three packs of cards, two penknives, the dancing doll, a Minnie Mouse, ornaments. He swivelled the crane about when he got the necklace for her, asking her what she wanted next, but this time the teeth closed an instant too soon and the bangle he'd gone after moved only slightly and then slipped back. They spent an hour in the Gold Mine.

'Go back to the bus station for a while?' he suggested, and Jasmin said she didn't mind. But on the way there were some seats, one on each side of a small concrete space with a concrete trough of shrubs in the middle. The shrubs were mostly dead, but one of the seats was empty and he asked her if she'd like to sit there.

'Yeah, it's nice,' Jasmin said.

An elderly man, asleep, was stretched out on the seat opposite the empty one. On another, a mother and her children were eating chips. On the third two women, in silence, stared at nothing.

'I come here when it's sunny,' the man Jasmin was with said. 'Nothing better to do, I come here.'

He'd made her wear the necklace, putting it on for her, the tips of his fingers cool on her neck as he fiddled with the clasp. He'd said it suited her. It suited her eyes, he'd said, and she wondered about that, the beads being yellowish. When they'd been going towards the machine that took you to the stars he'd said he was twenty-nine and she'd wanted to say she liked his being older, and almost did.

'The sun all right for you, Jasmin?'

The two women looked at them, one and then the other, still not speaking. The mother scolded her children when they asked for more chips. She bundled the empty cartons into a wastebin and they went away.

'There's vitamins in the sun. You know that, Jasmin?'

She nodded, although she hadn't been aware of this. She tried to look at her necklace but she couldn't see it properly when she pulled it taut and squinted down at the beads. If she'd been alone she would have taken it off, but she didn't like to do that now.

'Jasmin's a great name,' he said. On the chat line he had said that, complimenting her, although he didn't know she had given herself the name. She'd often thought he was affectionate when they had their conversations on the chat line, even though she'd been puzzled a few times when he described the telephone box he was in or read out what was written on a wall. The first time he'd read something out without saying he was doing it she'd wondered if he was all there in the head, but then he explained and it was all right. She imagined him in the courts, like you'd see on TV. She imagined him standing up with papers in one hand, putting a case. She imagined him looking to where she was watching, and his smile coming on, and wanting to wave at him but knowing she mustn't because he'd have told her that. The first time on the chat line he'd commented on her voice. 'You take it easy now,' he'd said, and she hung on because she didn't want him to go. 'Love that voice,' he said, and she realized he meant hers.

He was smiling at her now and they watched the sleeping man waking up. He had made a pillow of a plastic carrier-bag stuffed full of what might have been clothes. He had undone his shoelaces and he did them up again. He looked about him and then he went away.

'I thought you might say no, Jasmin, when I put it to you we'd meet up. Know what I mean, Jasmin? That you wouldn't want to take it further.'

She shook her head, denying that. She wanted her mother to go by, coming back from the betting shop, where the man Holby didn't know about worked. Holby was pathetic, her mother said, another mistake she'd made, same's the one with Jasmin's father. She had got into a relationship with the betting-shop man and the next thing would be he'd be a mistake too, no way he wouldn't.

'I'd never,' Jasmin heard herself protesting. 'I'd never have said no.'

She shook her head to make certain he was reassured. He'd lowered his voice when he'd said he had worried in case she'd say no. She didn't want anything spoiled; she wanted everything to go on being as good as on the chat line, as good as it was now.

'You at a loose end, Jasmin? You got the time today, come round to my place?'

Again there was the ripple of excitement. She could feel it all over her body, a fluttering of pins and needles it almost felt like but she knew it wasn't that. She loved being with him; she'd known she would. 'Yeah,' she said, not hesitating, not wanting him to think she had. 'Yeah, I got the time today.'

'Best to walk,' he said. 'All right with a walk, Jasmin?'

'Course I am.' And because it seemed to belong now, Jasmin added that she didn't know his name.

'Clive,' he said.

★

He liked that name and often gave it. Usually they asked, sometimes even on the chat line, before they got going. Rodney he liked too. Ken he liked. And Alistair.

'I never knew a Clive,' she said.

'You're living at home, Jasmin?'

'Oh, yes.'

'You said. A bit ago you said that. I only wondered if you'd moved out by now.'

'I wish I'd be able to.'

'Arm's length, are they?'

She didn't understand and he said her mother and whoever. On the chat line he remembered she'd said she was an only child. Her mother she'd mentioned then, the man she'd referred to in the bus station. He asked about him, wondering if he was West Indian, and she said yes. Light-coloured, she said. 'He passes.'

They had turned out of the busy streets, into Blenheim Row, leading to Sowell Street, where the lavatories were, the school at the end.

'A West Indian kid got killed here,' he said. 'White

kids took their knives out. You ever see a thing like that, Jasmin?'

'No.' Vehemently, she shook her head, and he laughed and then she did.

'You ever think of moving out, Jasmin? Anything like that come into your thoughts? Get a place of your own?'

All the time, she said. The only thing was, she wasn't earning.

'First thing you said to me nearly, that you'd got nothing coming in.'

'You're easy to talk with, Clive.'

He took her hand; she didn't object. Her fingernails were silvery he'd noticed in the McDonald's, a couple of them jagged where they'd broken. No way she wasn't a child, no way she'd reached sixteen, more like twelve. Her hand was warm, lying there in his, dampish, fingers interlaced with his.

'There used to be a song,' he said. '"Putting on the agony" was how it went. "Putting on the style". Before your time, Jas. It could have been called something else, only those were the words. "That's what all the young folk are doin' all the while". Lovely song.'

'Maybe I heard it one time, I don't know.'

'What age really, Jas?'

'Seventeen.'

'No, really though?'

She said fifteen. Sixteen in October, she said.

\*

When they were passing the Queen and Angel he asked her if she ever took a drink. It wouldn't do for him to bring her on to licensed premises, he explained, and she said she wasn't fussy for a drink, remembering the taste of beer, which she hadn't liked. He said to wait and he went to an off-licence across the street and came back with a plastic bag. He winked at her and she laughed. 'Mustn't be bad boys,' he said. 'No more than a few sips.'

They came to a bridge over the river. They didn't cross it, but went down steps to a towpath. He said it was a shortcut.

There wasn't anyone around, and they leaned against a brick wall that was part of the bridge. He unscrewed the cap of the bottle he'd bought and showed her how the plastic disc he took from one of his jacket pockets opened out to become a tumbler. Tonic wine, he said, but he had vodka too, miniatures he called the little bottles he had. What the Russians drank, he said, although she knew. He said he'd been in Moscow once.

They drank from the tumbler when he'd tasted the mixture he'd made and said it wasn't too strong. He'd never been responsible for making any girl drunk, he said. He had found the collapsible tumbler on the same seat where they'd been sitting in the sun. One day he'd seen it there and thought it was a powder compact. He carried it about with him in case he met a friend who'd like a drink.

'All right, Jas?'

'Yeah, great.'

'You like it, Jas?'

They passed the tumbler back and forth between them. She drank from where his lips had been; she wanted to do that. He saw her doing it and he smiled at her.

Nice in the sun, he said when they walked on, and he took her hand again. She thought he'd kiss her, but he didn't. She wanted him to. She wanted to sit on a patch of grass and watch the rowers going by, his arm round her shoulders, his free hand holding hers. There was some left in the bottles when he dropped them and the plastic bag into a wastebin.

'Sit down, will we?' she said, and they did, her head pressed into his chest. 'I love you, Clive,' she whispered, not able to stop herself.

'We belong,' he whispered back. 'No way we don't, Jas.'

She didn't break the silence when they walked on, knowing that it was special, and better than all the words there might have been. No words were necessary, no words could add a thing to what there was.

'I can see us in Moscow, Jas. I can see us walking the streets.'

She felt different, as if her plainness wasn't there. Her face felt different, her body too. In the diner she'd be a different person clearing up the plates, not minding the lorrymen's cigarette smoke, not minding what they said to her. Nothing she knew would be the same, her mother wouldn't be, and letting Lukie Giggs touch her where he wanted to wouldn't be. She wondered if she was drunk.

'You're never drunk, Jas.' He squeezed her hand, he

said she was fantastic. Both of them were only tipsy, he said. Happy, he said. Soon's he heard her voice he knew she was fantastic. Soon's he saw her at the bus station. In the room they were going to there were the things he collected – little plastic tortoises, and racing cars, and books about places he wanted to go to, and pictures of castles on the walls. She imagined that when he told her, and saw a vase of summer flowers, curtains drawn against the sunlight. He played a disc for her, the Spice Girls because they were in the past and he liked all that.

They turned off the towpath into a lane with a row of garage doors running along it, and walled back gardens on the other side. They came out on to a suburban road, and crossed it to a crescent. He dropped her hand before they reached it and pulled down the back of his jacket where it had ridden up a bit. He buttoned all three buttons.

'Would you wait five minutes, Jas?'

It was as if she knew about that, as if she knew why she had to wait and why it should be five minutes, as if he'd told her something she'd forgotten. She knew he hadn't. It didn't matter.

'You be all right, Jas?'

'Course I will.'

She watched him walking off and when he reached a front gate painted blue. She watched him as she had when he crossed the street to the off-licence. She waited, as she had waited then too, seeing again the little tortoises and the racing cars, hearing the Spice Girls. Across the road a delivery van drew up. No one got out, and a minute or so later it drove off. A dog went by. A woman started a lawnmower in one of the front gardens.

She waited for longer than he'd said, for ages it felt like, but when he came back he was hurrying, as if he was making up for that. He almost ran, his flannel trousers flapping. He was out of breath when he reached her. He shook his head and said they'd best go back.

'Back?'

'Best to go back, Jas.'

He took her arm, but he was edgy and didn't take it as he had before. He didn't search for her hand. He pulled her anorak when it was difficult for her to keep up with him. Behind them somewhere a car door banged.

'Oh God,' he said.

A red car slowed down beside them as they were turning into the lane with the garage doors. When it stopped a woman with glasses on a string around her neck got out. She was wearing a brown skirt, and a cardigan that matched it over a pale silk blouse. Her dark hair was coiled round her head, her lipstick glistened, as if she hadn't had time to powder it over or had forgotten to. The glasses bobbed about on her blouse and then were still. Her voice was angry when she spoke but she kept it low, giving the impression that her teeth were clenched.

'I don't believe this,' she said.

She spoke as if Jasmin wasn't there. She didn't look at her, not even glancing in her direction.

'For God's sake!' she almost shouted, and slammed the door of the car shut, as if she had to do something, as if only noise could express what she felt. 'For God's sake, after all we've been through!'

Her face was quivering with rage, one hand made into a fist that struck the roof of the car once and then opened, to fall by her side. There was silence then.

'Who is she?' The woman spoke when the silence had gone on, at last recognizing Jasmin's presence. Her question came wearily, in a bleak, dull tone. 'You're on probation,' she said. 'Did you forget somehow that you were on probation?'

The man whom she abused had not attempted to speak, had made no protestation, but words were muttered now.

'She was looking for the towpath. She asked me where it was. I don't know who she is.'

The long, peaky features might never that afternoon, or any afternoon, have been other than they had become in the brief time that had passed: devoid of all expression, dead, a dribble of tears beginning.

Then Jasmin's companion of so many conversations, and whom she had begun to love, shambled off, and the woman said nothing until he reached the blue-painted ornamental gate and again disappeared around the side of the house.

'Was there anything?' she asked then. She stared at Jasmin. Slowly she looked her up and down. Jasmin didn't know what her question meant.

'Did he do anything to you?' the woman asked, and Jasmin understood and yet did not. What mattered more was that he had cried, his happiness taken from him, his smile too. He had cried for her. He had cried for both of them. All that she understood too well.

'Who are you?' the woman asked. Her clenched-back voice, deprived of the energy of its anger, was frightened, and fear clung to the tiredness in her face.

'Clive's my friend,' Jasmin said. 'There wasn't nothing wrong. We done nothing wrong.'

'That's not his name.'

'Clive, he said.'

'He says anything. Did he give you drink?'

Jasmin shook her head. Why should she say? Why should she get him into trouble?

'You reek of drink,' the woman said. 'Every time he gives them drink.'

'He done nothing.'

'His mother was my sister. He lives with us.'

If she'd asked him, Jasmin said, he would have explained about his name. But the woman just stared at her when she began to tell her that she, also, had given herself a name, that sometimes people wanted to.

'My sister died,' the woman said. 'He's been living with us since that. He thought the house would be empty this afternoon but it wasn't because I changed my mind about going out. You worry and you change your mind. Quite often you do. Well, naturally, I suppose. He's been on charges.'

'He was only going to show me, like, where it is he lived.'

'What's your name?'

'Jasmin.'

'If this is known they'll take him in again.'

Jasmin shook her head. There was a mistake, she said. The woman said there wasn't.

'We look after him, we lie for him, my husband and I. We've done our best since my sister died. A family thing, you do your best.'

'There wasn't anything.'

'My sister knew his chance would come. She knew there'd be a day that would be too terrible for her to bear. He was her child, after all, it was too much. She left a note.'

'Honestly, I promise you.'

'I know, I know.'

The woman got into her car and wound the window down as if she intended to say something else but she said nothing. She turned in the quiet road and drove back to her house.

\*

Frying chops, Holby prodded them occasionally with a fork. He liked to blacken them, to see the smoke rising while still not turning down the gas. It got into her hair, Jasmin's mother maintained. Smoke like that was greasy, she insisted, but Holby said it couldn't be. He heard the door when Jasmin came into the kitchen and he called out to her, knowing it wasn't her mother who'd come in.

'How you doing, girl?'

All right, Jasmin said, and then her mother was there,

back from her time with her betting-shop friend. Even through the smoke, her entrance brought a gush of the perfume she so lavishly applied when she met her men.

'What're you frying, Holby?' She shouted above the sizzling of the meat, and Jasmin knew there was going to be a quarrel.

In her room, even with the door closed she heard it beginning, her mother's noisy criticisms, Holby's measured drone of retaliation. She didn't listen. Probably he had guessed at last about the betting-shop man, as her father had once guessed about him. Probably it had come to that – the frying of the chops, the smoke, the grease no more than a provocation, a way of standing up for himself. And Holby – today or some other day – would walk out, saying no man could stand it, which Jasmin remembered her father saying too.

She pulled the curtains over and lay down on her bed. She liked the twilight she had induced; even on better days than this she did. Tired after the walk to the house with the man she had begun to love, and after that the walk alone to where she lived herself, she closed her eyes. 'You like to go in here?' he asked again. He carried her coffee to where she waited. She felt the touch of his fingers when he put the necklace on for her. 'The sun all right for you?' he said.

In the room she still had to imagine there were books on shelves, the vase of flowers, the pictures of castles. In a courtroom he put a case, his papers in one hand, gesturing with the other. They belonged, he said on the towpath, the rowers going by.

Downstairs something was thrown, and there was Holby's mumble, the clank of broken china when it was swept up, her mother's voice going on, her crossness exhausted as the woman's had been. He had been shamed by the woman getting things wrong and was the kind to mind. He didn't realize the woman didn't matter, that her talk and her fury didn't. He wasn't the kind to know that. He wasn't the knowing sort.

Her mother's voice was different now, caressing, lying. She sent Holby out for beer, which at this stage in the proceedings she always did; Jasmin heard him go. Her mother called up the stairs, calling her Angie, saying to come down. She didn't answer. She didn't say that Angie wasn't her name. She didn't say anything.

When she went there, he would not be on the seat in the sun. He would not be waiting in the bus station. Nor playing the machines. Nor in the McDonald's. But when Jasmin closed her eyes again his smile was there and it didn't go away. She touched with her lips the necklace that had been his gift. She promised she would always keep it by her.

# At Olivehill

'Well, at least don't tell him,' their mother begged. 'At least do nothing until he's gone.'

But they were doubtful and said nothing. They did not promise, which she had hoped they would. Then, sensing her disappointment, they pacified her.

'We'd never want to distress him,' Tom said, and Eoghan shook his head.

She wasn't reassured, but didn't say. She knew what they were thinking: that being old you might be aware of death loitering near, but even so death wasn't always quick about its business. And she hated what had been said to her, out of the blue on such a lovely day.

She was younger by a year than their father, and who could say which would be taken first? Both of them suffered a raft of trivial ills, each had a single ailment that was more serious. In their later seventies, they lived from day to day.

'We'll say nothing so,' she said, still hoping they would promise what she wished for. 'Promise me,' she used to say when they were boys, and obediently they always had. But everything was different now. She knew they were doing all they could to keep things going. She knew it was a struggle at Olivehill.

'Don't be worrying yourself,' Eoghan said, his soft blue

eyes guilty for a moment. He was given to guilt, she thought. More than Tom was, more than Angela.

'It's just we have to look ahead,' Tom said. 'We have to see where we're going.'

They were having tea outside for the first time that summer although the summer was well advanced. The grass of the big lawn had been cut that morning by Kealy, the garden chairs brushed down. What remained of tea, the tablecloth still spread, was on the white slatted table, beneath which two English setters dozed.

'It'll be cold. I'll make some fresh,' she said when her husband came.

'No. No such thing.' Still yards away and advancing slowly, James contradicted that. 'You'll rest yourself, lady.'

Having heard some of this, she nodded obligingly. Both of them disregarded a similar degree of deafness and in other ways, too, were a little alike: tall but less tall than they had been, stooped and spare. Their clothes were not new but retained a stylishness: her shades of dark maroon, her bright silk scarf, his greenish tweeds, his careful tie. Their creeper-covered house, their garden here and there neglected, reflected their coming down in the world, but they did not themselves.

'Thanks, Mollie,' the old man said when his wife uncovered his toast, folding away the napkin so that it could be used for the same teatime purpose again. His toast was cut into tidy rectangles, three to a slice, and buttered. No one else had toast at this time of day.

'You're turning the hay?' He addressed both sons at

once, which was a habit with him. 'End of the week you'll bring it in, you think?'

Before Thursday, they said, when there might be a change in the weather. They were more casually turned out, in open-necked white shirts and flannel trousers, working farmers both of them. Tom and his family lived in a house on their land that once had been an employee's. When he could, which wasn't every day, he came to Olivehill at this time to be with the old couple for an hour or so. Once in a while his wife, Loretta, came too and brought the children. Eoghan wasn't married and still lived at Olivehill.

Spreading lemon curd on his toast, James wondered why both his sons were here at teatime; usually Eoghan wasn't when Tom came. He didn't ask, it would come out: what change they proposed, what it was that required the arguments of both to convince him. But in a moment Eoghan went away.

'You're looking spry,' Tom complimented his father.

'Oh, I'm feeling spry.'

'Fine weather's a tonic,' Mollie said.

And James asked after Loretta, which he always did, and asked about his granddaughters.

'They have the poor girl demented with their devilment.' Tom laughed, although it wasn't necessary, it being known that his demure daughters, twins of four, hadn't yet reached their mischievous years.

They were an Irish Catholic family, which once had occupied a modest place in an ascendancy that was not Catholic and now hardly existed any more. When Mollie first lived in this house the faith to which she and James belonged connected them with the nation that had newly come about. But faith's variations mattered less in Ireland all these years later, since faith itself mattered less and influenced less how people lived.

'Angela wrote,' Mollie said, finding the letter she'd brought to the garden to show Tom.

He read it and commented that Angela didn't change.

'Her men friends do rather,' James said.

Angela was the youngest of the children, a buyer for a chain of fashion shops. She lived in Dublin. The one that got away, Tom often said.

He and Eoghan hadn't wanted to. They still didn't, feeling they belonged here, content to let Angela bring a bit of life into things with her Dublin gossip and her flightiness.

Tom folded the letter into its envelope and handed it back. James slowly finished his tea. Mollie walked round the garden with her older son.

'You're good to indulge me, Tom,' she said, even though she had hoped to hear that what had been kept from their father would not come about at all. It made no sense to her that the greater part of Olivehill should be made into a golf-course in the hope that this would yield a more substantial profit than the land did. It was foolish, Mollie thought after Tom had gone, when she and James were alone again with the setters; yet her sons weren't fools. It was graceless, even a vulgarity, she thought as they sat there in the evening sun, for no other word was quite as suitable; yet they were not vulgar.

'Are we at one?' she heard James ask, and she apologized for being abstracted.

He loved to use that old expression. He loved to be reassured, was reassured now. How profoundly he would hate what she had protected him from, how chilling and loathsome it would seem to him, how disappointing.

'You're looking lovely,' he said, and she heard but pretended not to so that he'd say it again.

*

Eoghan drove carelessly to the hayfield. There never was other traffic on these byroads, never a lost cyclist or someone who had walked out from Mountmoy. A wandering sheep was always one of their own. But there wasn't a sheep today, only now and again a rabbit scuttling to safety.

You could sleep driving here, Eoghan used to say and once, in the heat of an afternoon, had dropped off at the turn to Ana Woods. He'd woken up before the old Austin he had then hit a tree. Not that it would have mattered much if he hadn't, he always added when he told the story: all the cars he had ever owned were past their best, purchased from Chappie Keogh, who had the wrecking yard at Maire. Easygoing, good-hearted, seeming to be slow but actually rather clever, Eoghan had grown from being a sensitive child into a big, red-haired man, different in appearance from the others of his family, all of whom were noticeably thin. He was content to take second place to Tom. They had all their lives been friends, their friendship knitted closer in each succeeding span of years.

He drove in to where earlier he'd been turning the hay. He finished it within an hour, not hurrying because he never did. Then he went on, to Brea Maguire's at the cross, where he drank and talked to the men who came there every evening. It would be a bad mistake, disastrous even, to go on doing nothing about Olivehill. They had wanted her to understand that, and hoped she did.

\*

Nine days later James woke up one morning feeling different, and had difficulty on the stairs. His left leg was dragging a bit, a most uncomfortable business, and at breakfast he discovered that his left arm was shaky too. Reaching out was limited; and he couldn't lift things as easily as he used to. 'A little stroke,' Dr Gorevan said when he came.

'Should he be in his bed?' Mollie asked, and James said he'd no intention of taking to his bed so Dr Gorevan prescribed instead a walking-stick. When she heard, Loretta came over with a sponge cake.

James died. Not then, but in the winter and of pneumonia. There had not been another stroke and he was less incapacitated than he had been at first from the one he'd had. A fire was kept going in his bedroom, and the family came often, one by one, to talk to him. But he was tired and, two days after his eightieth birthday, when the moment came he was glad to go. It was a good death: he called it that himself.

\*

In the house to which Mollie had come when she was a girl of nineteen, where there'd been servants and where later her children were born, there was only Kitty Broderick now, and Kealy was the last of the outside men. In the bleak dining-room Mollie and Eoghan sat at either end of the long mahogany table and Kitty Broderick brought them the meals she cooked. Everywhere there was the quiet that comes after death, seeming to Mollie to keep at bay what had been withheld from James. But one evening after supper, when the days had already lengthened and there was an empty hour or so, Eoghan said: 'Come and I'll show you.'

She went, not immediately knowing what for; had she known she would have demurred. Well, anyone would, she thought, passing from field to field.

'You can't do this, Eoghan,' she protested, having been silent, only listening.

'We wouldn't if there was another way.'

'But Ana Woods, Eoghan!'

They could go on selling timber piecemeal, as had been done in the past, another half-acre gone and replanted every so often, but that hadn't ever been a solution, and wasn't a way now in which the family could recover itself. It would tide the family over, but tiding-over wasn't what was needed. The woods were part of the whole and the whole had to be put right. Doing so on the scale that was necessary meant that the machinery for such an undertaking could be hired at more favourable rates. With more timber to offer it would fetch what it should, not dribs and drabs that added up to nothing much. And the well-cleared land could be put to profitable use. Eoghan explained all that.

'The Bluebell Walk, though, Eoghan! The beeches, the maples!'

'I know. I know.'

They went back through the yards and sat down in the kitchen. The setters, who had accompanied them in the fields and were not allowed in the kitchen regions, ambled off into another part of the house.

'For a long time,' Eoghan said, 'there's been waste. Papa knew that too.'

'He did his best.'

'He did.'

Parcels of land had been sold in much the same small way as timber had, a source of funds when need arose. Everything higgledy-piggledy, Eoghan said, the distant future forgotten about. It was an irony for Mollie that James, aware that he'd inherited a run-down estate, had struggled to put things right. The agricultural subsidies of the nineteen eighties and nineties were the saviour of many farms and were a help at Olivehill too, but they were not enough to reverse generations of erosion and mismanagement. 'It's maybe we're old stock ourselves,' James had said when he became resigned to defeat. 'It's maybe that that's too much for us.'

Often Mollie had heard this tale of woe repeated, although always privately, never said in front of the children. In his later life James's weariness marked him, as optimism had once. At least the furniture and the pictures were not sold, faith kept with better times.

'It's hard,' Eoghan said. 'I know all this is hard, Mamma.' He reached out for her hand, which Tom would have been shy of doing, which Angela might have in a daughterly way.

'It's only hard to imagine,' she said. 'So big a thing.'

They could keep going in a sort of way, Eoghan said. Tom and his family would come to live at Olivehill, the house they were in now offered to whoever replaced Kealy when the time for that arrived. A woman could come in a few mornings a week when Kitty Broderick went, economies made to offset any extra expense.

'But Tom's right,' Eoghan said, 'when he's for being more ambitious. And bolder while we're at it.'

She nodded, and said she understood, which she did not. The friendship of her sons, their respect for one another, their confidence in their joint ventures had always been a pleasure for her. It was something, she supposed, that all that was still there.

'And Angela?' she asked.

'Angela's aware of how things are.'

That night Mollie dreamed that James was in the drawing-room. 'No, no, no,' he said, and laughed because it was ridiculous. And they went to the Long Field and were going by the springs where men from the county council had sheets of drawings spread out and were taking measurements. 'Our boys are pulling your leg,' James told them, but the men didn't seem to hear and said to one another that Mountmoy wouldn't know itself with an amenity golf-course.

Afterwards, lying awake, Mollie remembered James telling her that the Olivehill land had been fought for, that during the penal years the family had had to resort to chicanery in order to keep what was rightfully theirs. His father had grown sugar beet and tomatoes at the personal request of de Valera during the nineteen forties' war. And when she dreamed again James was saying that in an age of such strict regulations no permission would be granted for turning good arable land into a golf-course. History was locked into Olivehill, he said, and history in Ireland was preciously protected. He was angry that his sons had allowed the family to be held up to ridicule, and said he knew for a fact that those county-council clerks had changed their minds and were sniggering now at the preposterousness of a naïve request.

\*

'We mustn't quarrel,' Eoghan said.

'No, we mustn't quarrel.'

She had been going to tell him her dream but she didn't. Nor did she tell Tom when he came at teatime. He was the sharper of the two in argument and always had been; but he listened, and even put her side of things for her when she became muddled and was at a loss. His eagerness for what he'd been carried away by in his imagination was unaffected while he helped her to order her objections, and she remembered him – fair-haired and delicate, with that same enthusiasm – when he was eight.

'But surely, Tom,' she began again.

'It's unusual in a town the size of Mountmoy that there isn't a golf-course.'

She didn't mention permission because during the day she had realized that that side of things would already have been explored; and this present conversation would be different if an insurmountable stumbling-block had been encountered.

'In the penal years, Tom –'

'That past is a long way off, Mamma.'

'It's there, though.'

'So is the future there. And that is ours.'

She knew it was no good. They had wanted their father's blessing, which they would not have received, but still they had wanted to try for it and perhaps she'd been wrong to beg them not to. His anger might have stirred their shame and might have won what, alone, she could not. That day, for the first time, her protection of him felt like betrayal.

At the weekend Angela came down from Dublin, and wept a little when they walked in the woods. But Angela wasn't on her side.

★

The front avenue at Olivehill was a mile long. Its iron entrance gates, neglected for generations, had in the end been sold to a builder who was after something decorative for an estate he had completed, miles away, outside Limerick. The gates' two stone pillars were still in place at Olivehill, and the gate-lodge beside them was, though fallen into disrepair. Rebuilt, it would become the clubhouse; and gorse was to be cleared to make space for a car park. A man who had designed golf-courses in Spain and South Africa came from Sussex and stayed a week at Olivehill. A planning application for the change of use of the gate-lodge had been submitted; the widening of access to and from the car park was required. No other stipulations were laid down.

Mollie listened to the golf-course man telling her about the arrangements he had made for his children's education and about his wife's culinary successes, learning too that his own interest was water-wheels. She was told that the conversion of Olivehill into a golf-course was an imaginative stroke of genius.

'You understand what's happening, Kitty?' Mollie questioned her one-time parlourmaid, whose duties were of a general nature now.

'Oh, I have, ma'am. I heard it off Kealy a while back.'

'What's Kealy think of it then?'

'Kealy won't stay, ma'am.'

'He says that, does he?'

'When the earth-diggers come in he won't remain a day. I have it from himself.'

'You won't desert me yourself, Kitty?'

'I won't, ma'am.'

'They're not going to pull the house down.'

'I wondered would they.'

'No, no. Not at all.'

'Isn't it the way things are though? Wouldn't you have to move with the times?'

'Maybe. Anyway, there's nothing I can do, Kitty.'

'Sure, without the master to lay down the word, ma'am, what chance would there be for what anyone would do? You'd miss the master, ma'am.'

'Yes, you would.'

When February came Mollie took to walking more than she'd ever walked in the fields and in the woods. By March she thought a hiatus had set in because there was a quietness and nothing was happening. But then, before the middle of that month, the herd was sold, only a few cows kept back. The pigs went. The sheep were kept, with the hens and turkeys. There was no spring sowing. One morning Kealy didn't come.

*

Tom and Eoghan worked the diggers themselves. Mollie didn't see that because she didn't want to, but she knew where a start had been made. She knew it from what Eoghan had let drop and realized, too late, that she shouldn't have listened.

That day Mollie didn't go out of the house, not even as far as the garden or the yards. Had she been less deaf, she would have heard, from the far distance, rocks and stones clattering into the buckets of the diggers. She would have heard the oak coming down in the field they called the Oak Tree Field, the chain-saws in Ana Woods. A third digger had been hired, Eoghan told her, with a man taken on to operate it, since Kealy had let them down. She didn't listen.

It was noticed then that she often didn't listen these days and noticed that she didn't go out. She hid her joylessness, not wishing to impose it on her family. Why should she, after all, since she was herself to blame for what was happening? James would have had papers drawn up, he would have acted fast in the little time he'd had left, clear and determined in his wishes. And nobody went against last wishes.

'Come and I'll show you,' Eoghan offered. 'I'll take you down in the car.'

'Oh now, you're busy. I wouldn't dream of it.'

'The fresh air'd do you good, Mamma.'

She liked that form of address and was glad it hadn't been dropped, that 'master' and 'mistress' had lasted too. The indoor servants had always been given their full names at Olivehill, and Kitty Broderick still was; yard men and gardeners were known by their surnames only. Such were the details of a way of life, James had maintained – like wanting to be at one, which he himself had added to that list.

More and more as the days, and then weeks, of that time went by Mollie clung to the drawing-room. She read there, books she'd read ages ago; played patience there, and a form of whist that demanded neither a partner nor an opponent. Father Thomas came to her there.

When Kealy returned it was in the drawing-room he apologized. His small, flushed face, the smell of sweat and drink, his boots taken off so as not to soil the carpet, all told the story of his retreat from what was happening, so very different from Mollie's own retreat. He asked that she should put a word in for him with her sons and she said it wasn't necessary. She said to go and find them and tell them she wanted him to be given back the position he'd had as yard man for thirty-four years. In spite of his dishevelment he went with dignity, Mollie considered.

Every third weekend or so Angela came, and also offered a tour of what was being achieved, but Mollie continued to decline this, making it seem no more than a whim of old age that she did so. Tom came to the drawing-room after his day's work, to sit with her over a seven o'clock drink, and when his children asked if their grandmother had died too, they were brought to the drawing-room to see for themselves that this was not so.

The pictures that were crowded on the drawing-room walls were of family ancestors – not Mollie's own but often seeming now as if they were – and of horses and dogs, of the house itself before the creeper had grown, square and gaunt. Among the oil paintings there were a few watercolours: of the Bluebell Walk, the avenue in autumn, the garden. There were photographs too, of Angela and Tom and Eoghan, as babies and as children, of Mollie and James after their marriage, of similar occasions before this generation's time. The drawing-room was dark even at the height of summer; only at night, with all the lights on, did its record of places and people emerge from the shadowed walls. Rosewood and mahogany were identified then, bookcases yielded the titles of their books. Candlesticks in which candles were no longer lit, snuff-boxes that had become receptacles for pins were given back something of their due.

In this room Mollie had been in awe of James's father and of his mother, had thought they didn't take to her, had wondered if they considered the levity of her nature an unsuitable quality in a wife. The prie-dieu – still between the two long windows – had seemed too solemn and holy for a drawing-room, the reproduction of a Mantegna *Virgin and Child* on the wall above it too serious a subject. But since she had claimed the drawing-room as her sanctuary she often knelt at the prie-dieu to give thanks, for she had ceased, in the peace of not knowing, to feel torn between the living and the dead. Protecting James had not been a sin; nor was it a sin to choose a reality to live by that her mood preferred. There was no fantasy in her solace, no inclination to pretend – companionable and forgiving – the presence with her of her long-loved husband. Memory in its ordinary way summoned harvested fields, and haycocks and autumn hedges, the first of the fuchsia, the last of the wild sweet-pea. It brought the lowing of cattle, old donkeys resting, scampering dogs, and days and places.

In the drawing-room she closed imagination down, for it was treacherous and without her say-so would take her into the hostile territory. 'Oh, ma'am, you should see it!' Kitty Broderick came specially to tell her, and called all that there was to see a miracle. Ten years it would have taken once, Kealy said. Less than eighteen months it had taken now.

★

One day Mollie drew the curtains on the daylight and did not ever draw them back again. Her meals were brought to the drawing-room when she hinted that she would like that, and when she said that the stairs were getting a bit much her sons dismantled her bed and it was made up beside the prie-dieu. Father Thomas said Mass in the dimly lit room on Saturday evenings and sometimes the family came, Angela if she happened to be in the house, Loretta and the children. Kitty Broderick and Kealy came too, Mass at that time of day being convenient for them.

Tom was disconsolate about the turn of events, but Angela said their mother was as bright as a bee. She said allowances had to be made for ageing's weariness, for a widow's continuing sorrow, that being reclusive was really hardly strange.

Eoghan protested. 'What you're doing's not good, Mamma,' he chided.

'Ah now, Eoghan, ah now.'

'We don't want you to be against us.'

She shook her head. She said she was too old to be against people. And he apologized again.

'We had to, you know.'

'Of course you had to. Of course, Eoghan.'

*

The ersatz landscape took on a character of its own – of stumpy hillocks that broke the blank uniformity, long fairways, sandy bunkers, a marsh created to catch the unwary, flat green squares and little flags. *Olivehill Golf Links 1 Km*, a sign said, and later the golf-course's immediate presence was announced, the car park tarred, its spaces marked in white. Completion of the clubhouse dragged but then at last was finished. Niblicks flashed in the sun of another summer. Mountmoy boys learned how to be caddies.

*

In her meditative moments Mollie knew that James had been betrayed. His anger had not been allowed, nor had it become her own, for she could not have managed it. With good intentions, he had been deceived, and had he known he might have said the benevolence was as bitter as the treachery. He would have said – for she could hear him – that the awfulness which had come about was no more terrible, no less so either, than the impuissance of Catholic families in the past, when hunted priests were taken from their hiding-places at Olivehill and Mass was fearfully said in the house, when suspicion and distrust were everywhere. Yet through silence, with subterfuge, the family at Olivehill had survived, a blind eye turned to breaches of the law by the men who worked the fields, a deaf ear to murmurs of rebellion.

In the darkened drawing-room, as shielded as James was from the new necessities of survival, Mollie tentatively reflected what she believed he might have reflected himself. In that distant past, misfortune had surely brought confusion, as it had now – and disagreement about how to accept defeat, how best to banish pride and know humility, how best to live restricted lives. And it was surely true that there had been, then too, the anger of frustration; and guilt, and tired despair.

'I've brought your tea.' Kitty Broderick interrupted the flow of thought. Light from the door she'd left open allowed her to make her way safely into the room, to put the tray she carried down. She pulled the table it was on closer to where Mollie sat.

'You're good to me, Kitty.'

'Ach, not at all. Wouldn't I pull the curtains back a bit, though?'

'No. No, the curtains are grand the way they are. Didn't you bring a cup for yourself?'

'Oh, I forgot the cup!' She always did, was never at ease when the suggestion was made that she should sit down and share the mistress's tea.

'Kealy got drunk again,' she said.

'Is he all right?'

'I have him in the kitchen.'

'Kealy likes his glass.'

He wasn't as particular as Kitty Broderick, always

accepting when he came to the drawing-room the whis-key she kept specially for him. When Tom came in the evenings it was for sherry.

'How silent it can be, Kitty, in the drawing-room. Nearly always silent.'

'It's a quiet room, all right. Sure, it always was. But wouldn't you take a little walk, though, after your tea?'

The bluebells had begun to grow again. They'd told her that. Kitty Broderick knew she wouldn't go for a walk, that she wouldn't come out from where she belonged, and be a stranger on her own land. They'd wanted her to have the setters with her for company, but it wasn't fair to keep dogs closed up all day like that and she said no.

Nothing changed, she thought when the maid had gone; and after all why should it? Persecution had become an ugly twist of circumstances, more suited to the times. Merciless and unrelenting, what was visited on the family could be borne, as before it had been. In her artificial dark it could be borne.

# A Perfect Relationship

'I'll tidy the room,' she said. 'The least I can do.'

Prosper watched her doing it. She had denied that there was anyone else, repeating this several times because he had several times insisted there must be.

The cushions of the armchairs and the sofa were plumped up, empty glasses gathered. The surface of the table where the bottles stood was wiped clean of sticky smears. She had run the Hoky over the carpet.

It was early morning, just before six. 'I love this flat,' she used to say and, knowing her so well, Prosper could feel her wanting to say it again now that she was leaving it. But she didn't say anything.

Once, before she came to live here, they had walked in the Chiltern hills. Hardly knowing one another, they had stayed in farmhouses, walking from one to the next for the two nights of the weekend. He had identified birds for her – stone curlews, wheatears – and wild flowers when he knew what they were himself. She was still attending the night school then and they often talked to one another in simple Italian, which was one of the two languages he taught her there. She spelled *giochetto* and *pizzico* for him; she used, correctly, the imperfect tense. He wondered if she remembered that or if she remembered her shyness of that time, and her humility, and how she never forgot to thank him for things. And how she'd said he knew so much.

'I love you, Chloë.'

Dark-haired and slim, not tall, Chloë dismissed her looks as ordinary. But in fact her prettiness was touched with beauty. It was in the deep blue of her eyes, her perfect mouth, her profile.

'I hate doing this,' she said. 'It's horrible. I know it is.'

He shook his head, not in denial of what she said, only to indicate bewilderment. She had chosen the time she had – the middle of the night, as it had been – because it was easier then, almost a *fait accompli* when he returned from the night school, easier to find the courage. He guessed that, but didn't say it because it mattered so much less than that she didn't want to be here any more.

The muted colours of the clothes she was wearing were suitable for a bleak occasion, as if she had specially chosen them: the grey skirt she disliked, the nondescript silk scarf that hadn't been a present from him as so many other scarves were, the plain cream blouse he'd never seen without a necklace before. She looked a little different and perhaps she thought she should because that was how she felt.

'Where are you going, Chloë?'

Her back was to him. She tried to shrug. She picked a glass up and turned to face him when she reached the door. No one else knew, she said. He was the first to know.

'I love you, Chloë,' he said again.

'Yes, I do know that.'

'We've been everything to one another.'

'Yes.'

The affection in their relationship had been the pleasure of both their lives: that had not been said before in this room, nor even very often that they were fortunate. The reticence they shared was natural to them, but they knew – each as certainly as the other – what was not put into words. Prosper might have contributed now some part of this, but sensing that it would seem like protesting too much he did not.

'Don't,' he begged instead, and she gazed emptily at him before she went away.

He heard her in the bedroom when she finished with the Hoky in the hall. The telephone rang and she answered it at once; a taxi-driver, he guessed, for Clement Gardens was sometimes difficult to find.

Exhausted, Prosper sat down. Middle-aged, greying a little, his thin face anxious, as it often was, he wondered if he looked as disturbed and haggard as he felt. 'Don't,' he whispered. 'For God's sake, don't, Chloë.'

No sound came from the bedroom, either of suitcases and bags being zipped or of footsteps. Then the doorbell rang and there were voices in the hall, hers light and easy, polite as always, the taxi-man's a mumble. The door of the flat banged.

He sat where she had left him, thinking he had never known her, for what else made sense? He imagined her in the taxi that was taking her somewhere she hadn't told him about, even telling the taxi-driver more – why she was going there, what the trouble was. There had been no goodbye. She hadn't wept. 'I'm sorry,' was what she'd said when he came in from the night school more or less at the usual time. His hours were eight until half past one and he almost always stayed longer with someone who had fallen behind. He had this morning, and then had walked because he felt the need for fresh air, stopping as he often did for a cup of tea at the stall in Covent Garden. It was twenty to three when he came in and she hadn't gone to bed. It had taken her most of the night to pack.

Prosper didn't go to bed himself, nor did he for all that day. There hadn't been a quarrel. They had never quarrelled, not once, not ever. She would always cherish that, she'd said.

He took paracetamol for a headache. He walked about the flat, expecting to find she had forgotten something because she usually did when she packed. But all trace of her was gone from the kitchen and the bathroom, from the bedroom they had shared for two and a half years. In the afternoon, at half past four, a private pupil came, a middle-aged Slovakian woman, whose English he was improving. He didn't charge her. It wasn't worth it since she could afford no more than a pittance.

\*

All day Chloë's work had been a diversion. Now there was a television screen, high up in a corner, angled so that it could be seen without much effort from the bed. People she knew would have put her up for a while, but she hadn't wanted that. Breakfast was included in the daily rate at the Kylemore Hotel; and it was better, being on her own.

But the room she'd been shown when she came to make enquiries a week ago wasn't this one. The faded wallpaper was stained, the bedside table marked with cigarette burns. The room she'd been shown was clean at least and she'd hesitated when this morning she'd been led into a different one. But, feeling low, she hadn't been up to making a fuss.

From the window she watched the traffic, sluggish in congestion – taxis jammed, bus-drivers patient, their windows pulled open in the evening heat, cyclists skilfully manoeuvring. Still gazing down into the street, Chloë knew why she was here and reminded herself of that. But knowing, really, was no good. She had been happy.

*

It was the second time that Prosper had been left. The first time there had been a marriage, but the separation that followed the less formal relationship was no less painful; and in the days that now crawled by, anguish became an agony. He dreaded each return to the empty flat, especially in the small hours of the morning. He dreaded the night school, the chatter of voices between classes, the brooding presence of Hesse, who was its newly appointed principal, the hot-drinks machine that gave you what it had, not what you wanted, the class-room faces staring back at him. 'All right?' Hesse enquired, each guttural syllable articulated slowly and with care, his great blubber face simulating concern. In Prosper's dreams the contentment he had known for two and a half years held on and he reached out often to touch the companion who was not there. In the dark the truth came then, merciless, undeniable.

When that week ended he went to Winchelsea on the Sunday, a long slow journey by train and bus, made slower by weekend work on different stretches of the railway line.

'Well, this is nice,' her mother said, flustered when she opened the hall door.

She led him into the sitting-room he remembered from the only time he had been in this house before – the prints of country scenes on the walls, the ornaments, a bookcase packed with books that Chloë said had never been read. The fire was unlit because this morning the room was sunny. A black-and-white dog – reluctant when it was shooed out of the french windows – smelled as it had before, of damp or of itself. A Sunday that had been too.

'Oh yes, we've been well,' Chloë's mother said when she was asked. 'He has a new thing now.'

Metal-detecting this turned out to be, poking about with a gadget on Winchelsea beach, which was the best for this purpose for miles around. 'You'll have a cup of coffee? Or lunch? He'll be back for lunch.'

Prosper had always known she didn't like him, an older man and not a type she could take to: he could hear her saying it. And now he'd caught her with a curler in her wispy grey hair, forgotten, he supposed. He watched her realizing, a nervous gesture, fingers patting one side of her head. She left him on his own and came back saying she was sorry for deserting him. She offered sherry, the bottle almost empty.

'He said he'd get some more.' She poured out what there was, none for herself.

'I don't know where she is,' Prosper said. 'I thought she might be here.'

'Oh, Chloë's not here.'

'I wondered –'

'No, Chloë's not here.'

'I wondered if she said anything about where she is.'

'Well, no.'

He wondered what had been said, how it had been put, presumably on the telephone. He wondered if they'd been told more than he had himself, if they'd been glad, or at least relieved, both of them, not just she.

'He'll be back soon. He wouldn't like to miss you.'

Prosper believed that, seeing in his mind's eye the lanky figure prodding at the shingle of the beach with his detector. Her father had made a pet of Chloë and probably considered she could do no wrong; but even so it was he whom Prosper had come to see. It hadn't been the truth when he'd said he thought she might be here.

'It's difficult,' her mother said. 'In the light of everything, it's difficult.'

When she finished speaking she shook her head repeatedly. Prosper said he understood.

'He'd want to see you. He'd want me to invite you.'

'You're very kind.'

'He's never idle.'

'I remember that.'

'He made those ships in bottles all last winter. You see the ships, going through the hall?'

'Yes, I noticed the ships.'

'It's lamb I've got for today. A little leg, but it's enough.'

There was her husband's key in the front door while she spoke, then his voice called out to her, saying he was back.

\*

Chloë left the Kylemore Hotel that same Sunday morning and took a taxi to Maida Vale, where she laid her things out in the room she'd been lent while the girl who lived there was on holiday in Provence. It would be better than the hotel, and three weeks might just be long enough to find somewhere permanent.

She filled the drawers that had been allocated to her and hung what clothes there was room for in a hanging space behind a curtain. A stroke of luck she'd called it when the girl – an office colleague whom she didn't otherwise know – had suggested this arrangement, quoting the rent and requesting that it should be paid in advance. Chloë had lived in a quite similar room before she'd moved into the flat at Clement Gardens.

He hadn't pressed her to do that; at no stage had he done so, at no stage in their relationship had he ever pressed her about anything. As soon as she saw the flat she had wanted to be there, enraptured by its spaciousness, and the grandeur – so she called it – of Clement Gardens. The gardens themselves, where you could sit out in summer, were for the use of the tenants only, the rules that kept them peaceful strictly enforced.

She went out in search of coffee and found a café with pavement tables in the sun. She told herself she wasn't lonely, knowing that she was. Would weekends always be the worst? she wondered. The worst because they'd meant so much, even before she'd come to Clement Gardens, or perhaps particularly so then? She made a list of things to buy and asked the waitress who brought her coffee if there was somewhere open near by. 'Yeah, sure,' the waitress said, and told her where.

People exercising their dogs went by, children in the company of fathers claiming their Sunday access, dawdling couples. A church bell had begun to ring; the elderly, with prayer books, hurried. Resentment grumbled in the children's features, the fathers struggled with conversation.

For a moment, feeling sleepy in the sun, for she'd been restless in the night, Chloë dozed; and waking, in memory saw the woman who had been his wife. 'Prosper!' this beautiful person had called out from the crowd at the Festival Hall, still possessing him, a little, with her smile. And Chloë had wondered as they returned to their seats for the second part of the concert if the man who was tonight the companion of this woman was the one she had run away to, and imagined that he was.

She made her list of what she needed. Mahler's Fifth Symphony it had been, a CD of which had been played for weeks before she was taken to the Festival Hall. One composer at a time had been his way of bringing music into her life.

\*

Her father was shy, and made more so by what had happened. He was bent a little from the shoulders, which with his frailness made him seem older than he was, which was sixty-seven. 'I'm sorry,' he said when his wife was out of the room.

'I don't know why it happened.'

'Stay with us for lunch, Prosper.'

The invitation sounded almost compensatory, but Prosper knew he was imagining that, that nothing so ridiculous was intended.

'I don't know where she is.'

'I think she wants to be alone.'

'Could you –'

'No, we couldn't do that.'

They walked together to the Lord and Lady, which Prosper on that other Sunday had been taken to for a similar purpose: to bring back jugs of lunchtime beer.

'Have something now we're here?' the same offer came in the saloon bar and, remembering, her father ordered gin and tonic, and a Worthington for himself.

'We couldn't do something Chloë doesn't want us to,' he said while they waited for them.

There was a photograph of her framed on the sitting-room mantelpiece, a bare-footed child of nine or ten in a bathing dress, laughing among sandcastles that had been dotted around her in a ring. She hated that photograph, she used to say. She hated that sitting-room. They'd called her Chloë after a prim character in a film. She couldn't get to like the name.

'There's no one else,' Prosper said.

'Chloë told us there was nothing like that.'

The glass of beer was raised and Prosper did the same with his gin and tonic.

'There wasn't a quarrel,' he said.

'You did a lot for Chloë, Prosper. We know what you've done for her.'

'Less than it might seem.'

Teaching wasn't much, you passed on information. Anyone could have taken her to foreign films, anyone could have taken her to the National Gallery or told her who Apemantus was. She'd been the most perceptive and intelligent of all the girls he'd ever taught.

'I'll be honest with you, Prosper – at home here we haven't always seen eye to eye on the friendship. Not that we've ever come to fireworks. No, I don't mean that.'

'I'm an older man.'

'Yes, it's come up.'

'It hasn't made much of a difference. Not to Chloë. Not to either of us.'

A note of pleading kept creeping into Prosper's voice. He couldn't dispel it. He felt pathetic, a failure because he was unable to give a reason for what had happened. Why should they feel sorry for him? Why should they bother with a discarded man?

'Chloë's never been headstrong,' her father said. He sounded strained, as if the conversation was too much for him too.

'No,' Prosper said. 'No, she isn't that.'

Her father nodded, an indication of relief: a finality had been reached.

'You go there in the morning,' he said, 'you have the whole beach to yourself. Miles of it and you have it to yourself. It's surprising what you turn up. Well, there'll be nothing, you say. You're always wrong.'

'I shouldn't have come bothering you. I'm sorry.'

'No, no.'

'I've tried to find her. I've phoned round.'

'We'd best be getting back, you know.'

They said hardly anything on the walk to the house, and in the dining-room. Prosper couldn't eat the food that was placed before him. The silences that gathered lasted longer each time they were renewed and there was only silence in the end. He should have made her tell him where she was going, he said, and saw they were embarrassed, not commenting on that. When he left he apologized. They said they were sorry too, but he knew they weren't.

On the train he fell asleep. He woke up less than a minute later, telling himself the lunchtime beer on top of the gin and tonic had brought that about. It didn't mean there wasn't someone else just because she'd said it and had said it to them too, just because she never lied. Everyone lied. Lies were at everyone's disposal, waiting to be picked up when there was a use to put them to.

That there was someone else made sense of everything, some younger man telling her what to do.

The train crept into Victoria and he sat there thinking about that until a West Indian cleaner told him he should be getting off now. He pressed his way through the crowds at the station, wondering about going to one of the bars but deciding not to. He changed his mind again on the way to the Underground, not wanting to be in the flat. It took an hour to walk to the Vine in Wystan Street, where they had often gone to on Sunday afternoons.

It was quiet, as he'd known it would be. Voices didn't carry in the Vine and weren't raised anyway; in couples or on their own, people were reading the Sunday papers. He'd brought her here when she was still at the night school, after a Sunday-afternoon class. 'You saved me,' she used to say, and he remembered her saying it here. At the night school, crouched like a schoolgirl at her desk, obedient, humble, her prettiness unnourished, her cleverness concealed, she'd been dismissive of herself. Trapped by her nature, he had thought, and less so when their friendship had begun, when they had walked away from the night school together through the empty, darkened streets, their conversation at first about the two languages she was learning, and later about everything. Sometimes they stopped at the Covent Garden coffee stall, each time knowing one another better. An only child, her growing up was stifled; net curtains genteelly kept out the world. There was, for him in marriage, the torment of not being wanted any more. She was ashamed of being ashamed, and he was left with jealousy and broken pride. Their intimacy saved him too.

There was an empty table in the alcove of the wine bar, one they'd sat at. Hair newly hennaed, black silk clinging to her curves, Margo – who owned the place – waved friendlily from behind the bar.

'Chloë's not well,' he said when she came to take his order, her wrist chains rattling while she cleared away glasses and wiped the table's surface.

'Poor Chloë,' she murmured, and recommended the white Beaune, her whispery voice always a surprise, since her appearance suggested noisiness.

'She'll be all right.' He nodded, not knowing why he pretended. 'Just a half,' he said. 'Since I'm on my own.'

Someone else brought it, a girl who hadn't been in the bar before. Half-bottles of wine had a cheerless quality, he used to say, and he saw now what he had meant, the single glass, the stubby little bottle.

'Thanks,' he said, and the girl smiled back at him.

He sipped the chilled wine, glancing about at the men on their own. Any one of them might be waiting for her. That wasn't impossible, although it would have been once. A young man of about her age, a silk scarf casually tucked into a blue shirt open at the neck, dark glasses pushed up on to his forehead, was reading a paperback with the same cover as the edition Prosper possessed himself, *The Diary of a Country Priest*.

He tried to remember if he had ever recommended that book to her. *The Secret Agent* he'd recommended, and Poe and Louis Auchincloss. She had never read

Conrad before. She had never heard of Scott Fitzgerald, or Faulkner or Madox Ford.

The man had blond hair, quite long, but combed. A pullover, blue too, trailed over the back of his chair. His canvas shoes were blue.

He was the kind: Prosper hardly knew why he thought so, and yet the longer the thought was there the more natural it seemed that it should be. Had they noticed one another some other Sunday? Had he stared at her the way men sometimes do? When was it that a look had been exchanged?

He observed the man again, noted his glances in the direction of the door. A finger prodded the dark glasses further back, a bookmark was slipped between the pages of *The Diary of a Country Priest*, then taken out again. But no one came.

It was a green-and-black photograph on the book's cover, the young priest standing on a chair, the woman holding candles in a basket. Had the book been taken from the shelves in the flat, to lend a frisson of excitement, a certain piquancy, to deception? Again the dark glasses were pushed up, the bookmark laid on the table. People began to go, returning their newspapers to the racks by the door.

Suddenly she would be there. She would not notice that he was there too, and when she did would look away. The first time at the Covent Garden coffee stall she said that all her life she'd never talked to anyone before.

For a moment Prosper imagined that it had happened,

that she came and that the man reached out for her, that his arms held her, that she held him. He told himself he mustn't look. He told himself he shouldn't have come here, and didn't look again. At the bar he paid for the wine he hadn't drunk and on the street he cried, and was ashamed, hiding his distress from people going by.

★

She watched while twilight went, and while the dark intensified and the lights came on in the windows of the flat that overlooked the gardens. 'Oh, a man gets over it.' Her mother had been sure of that. Her mother said he'd be all right, her father that they'd gone together for the lunchtime beer. She had telephoned because he would have been there; she'd guessed he would. 'Never your type, he wasn't,' her mother said. Her father said stick by what she'd done. 'Cut up he is, but you were fair and clear with him.' Her mother said he'd had his innings.

Eventually they would say he wasn't much. Often disagreeing, they would agree because it made things easier if that falsity seemed to be the truth. 'Oh, long ago,' her mother would say, 'long ago I remarked to Dad it wasn't right.'

A shadow smudged one of the lighted windows, then wasn't there. The warm day had turned cold, but in the gardens the air was fresh and still. She was alone there now, and she remembered when he'd led her about among the shrubs before she came to live in the flat. 'Hibiscus,' he said when she asked, and said another was hypericum, another potentilla, another mahonia. She remembered the names, and imagined she always would.

When she left the gardens she pulled the gate behind her and heard the lock clicking. She crossed the street and stood in front of the familiar door. All she had to do was to drop the key of the gate into the letterbox: she had come to do that, having taken it away by mistake. It would be discovered in the morning under the next day's letters and put with them on the shelf in the hall, a found object waiting for whoever might have mislaid it.

But with the key in her hand, Chloë stood there, not wanting to give it up like this. A car door banged somewhere; faint music came from far away. She stood there for minutes that seemed longer. Then she rang the bell of the flat.

*

He heard her footsteps on the stairs when he opened the door. When he closed it behind her she held out the key. She smiled and did not speak.

'It's good of you,' he said.

He had known it was she before she spoke on the intercom. As if telepathy came into this, he had thought, but did not quite believe it had.

'You went down to the Coast.'

She always called it that – was never more precise – as if the town where she had lived deserved no greater distinction, sharing, perhaps, what she disliked about the house.

They had been standing and now sat down. Without asking, he poured her a drink.

'I have a room for a few weeks,' she said. 'I'll look round for somewhere.'

'It was just there may be letters to forward. And awkward if people ring up. Awkward, not knowing what to say.'

'I'm sorry.'

'Well, there haven't been letters so far. And no one has rung up. I shouldn't have gone to Winchelsea.'

'I should have told you more.'

'Why have you gone away, Chloë?'

*

Chloë heard herself answering that, in hardly more than a whisper saying she had been silly. And having said it she knew she had to say more, yet it was difficult. The words were there, and she had tried before. In the long evening hours, alone in the flat while he was at the night school, she had tried to string them together so that, becoming sentences, they became her feelings. But always they were severe, too cruel, not what she wanted, ungrateful, cold. In telling him, she did not mean to hurt, or to convey impatience or to blame. Wearied by introspection, night after night, she had gone to bed and slept; and woken sometimes when he returned, and then was glad to be there with him.

'I didn't know it was a silliness,' she said.

Friendship had drawn them together. Giving and

taking, they had discovered one another at a time when they were less than they became. She had always been aware of that and that it was enough, more than people often had. Still in search of somewhere to begin, she said so now. And added after a moment: 'I want to be here.'

He didn't speak. He wasn't looking at her, not that he had turned away, not that he resented her muddle, or considered that she should not have allowed it to come about: she knew this wasn't so, he had never been like that.

'I thought it would be easy,' she said.

There had been certainty. In her feelings she had been sure even when they were confused, even when she couldn't think because she'd thought too much and had exhausted reason. She had clung to her certainty, had sensed its truth: that she had lost, and was losing still, a little of herself. With kindness, and delighting her, her life had been arrested, while hungrily she accepted what was on offer. But her certainty was not there as soon as she was on her own.

'You make a mistake,' she said, 'and know it when you live with it.'

*

Prosper understood because he was quick to understand; and understanding nothing only moments ago, now understood too much. A calmness possessed him, the first time today there had been calmness, the first time since she had packed her things and gone away. He hadn't known there'd been misgivings.

He had been jealous in the wine bar: that was what happened when emotions rampaged out of control, what panic and distress could do. It was her fault, she said. No, it was no one's fault, he contradicted that.

She said he was forgiving. She said her mother's contempt was not meant, and that in time her father would be pleased. Mattering so much, he thought, that didn't matter now.

She made them scrambled eggs. They drank a little more, and the mood of relief being what it was for Chloë she celebrated their time together, recalling the Chilterns and their walks through the darkened streets in the early hours. And weekend visits to the cinema, her coming to the flat, their living there and never quarrelling, the gardens in summer.

Prosper didn't say much and nothing at all of what he might have, not wanting to, although he knew he must. The plates they'd eaten their scrambled eggs from remained on the coffee-table. Their glasses, not yet finished with, were there; her key to the gardens was. And they were shadows in the gloom, the room lit only by a single table-lamp.

Prosper didn't want the night to end. He loved her, she gave him back what she could: he had never not known that. Her voice, still reminiscing, was soft, and when it sounded tired he talked himself and, being with her, found the courage she had found and lost. His it was to order now what must be, to say what must be said. There had been no silliness, there wasn't a mistake.

# The Children

'We must go now,' Connie's father said and Connie didn't say anything.

The two men stood with their shovels, hesitating. Everyone else, including Mr Crozier, who had conducted the funeral service, had gone from the graveside. Cars were being started or were already being eased out of where they were parked, close to the church wall on the narrow road.

'We have to go, Connie,' her father said.

Connie felt in the pocket of her coat for the scarf-ring and thought for a moment she had lost it, but then she felt the narrow silver band. She knew it wasn't silver but they had always pretended. She leaned forward to drop it on to the coffin and took the hand her father held out to her. By the churchyard gate they caught up with the last of the mourners, Mrs Archdale and the elderly brothers, Arthur and James Dobbs.

'You'll come to the house,' her father invited them in case an invitation hadn't already been passed on to them. But people knew: the cars that were slipping away were all going in the same direction, to the house three and a quarter miles away, still just within the townland of Fara.

Connie would have preferred this to be different. She would have liked the house to be quiet now and had imagined, this afternoon, her father and herself gathering up her mother's belongings, arranging them in whatever way the belongings of the dead usually were arranged, her father explaining how they should be as they went along. She had thought of them alone after the funeral, doing all this because it was the time for it, because that was something you felt.

Her mother's dying, and the death itself, had been orderly and anticipated. Connie had known for months that it would come, for weeks that she would throw her scarf-ring on to the coffin at the very last minute. 'Brown Thomas's,' her mother had said when she was asked where it had been bought, and had given it to Connie because she didn't want it herself any more. This afternoon, in the quiet bedroom, there would be other things: familiar brooches, familiar earrings, and clothes and shoes, of course; odds and ends in drawers. But she and her father were up to that.

'All right, Connie?' he asked, turning left instead of taking the Knocklofty road, which was the long way round.

There'd been no pain; that had been managed well. While she was at the hospice, and when she came home at the end because suddenly she wanted to, you could tell that there had been no pain. 'Because we prayed for that, I suppose,' Connie had said when everything was over, and her father said he supposed so too. More important than anything it was that there had been no pain.

'Oh, I'm OK,' she said.

'They have to come to the house. They won't stay long.'

'I know.'

'You've been a strength, Connie.'

He meant it. He himself had been the source of strength at first and had seen her through that time, before she began to give back what he had given her. She had adored her mother.

'She would want us to be hospitable,' he said, unnecessarily, saying too much.

'I know we have to be.'

Connie was eleven and had her mother's faded blue eyes, and hair the colour of corn-stalks, as her mother's had been too. The freckles on her forehead and on the bridge of her nose were a feature of her own.

'We can get down to it when they've gone,' she said as they drove on, past the two cottages where nobody lived, down the hill that suddenly became almost dark, beech foliage meeting overhead. Mrs Archdale had been given a lift by the Dobbs brothers, their red Ford Escort already turning in at the gates. On the uneven surface of the avenue other cars were progressing cautiously, watched by the fenced sheep on either side.

'Come in, come in,' Connie's father invited the mourners who had already left their cars and were conversing in quiet tones on the gravel in front of the house. He was a tall, thin man, dark hair beginning to go grey, a boniness distinguishing his features. Sombrely dressed today, he was quite notably handsome. He had known much longer than his child had that his wife was going to die, but always at first there had been hope of a kind. Connie had been told when there was none.

The hall door wasn't locked. He'd left it so, wanting people to go in as soon as they arrived, but no one had. He pushed it open and stood aside. All of them would know the way and Mrs O'Daly would be there, tea made.

\*

When Teresa was left by her husband she'd felt humiliated by the desertion. 'You'll have them to yourself,' he'd said; with ersatz gentleness, she considered. 'I promise you I won't be a nuisance about that.' He spoke of their two children, whom she had always believed were fonder of him than they were of her. And it seemed wrong that they should be deprived of him: in her lowness at the time she had even said so, had felt she should be punished further for her failure to keep a marriage together, should lose them too. 'Oh no,' he had protested. 'No, I would never do that.'

Among the mourners in the drawing-room, she remembered that with poignancy, wondering if the pain of death so early in a marriage left behind the same cruel rawness that did not change and lingered for so long. 'I'm sorry,' she said when Connie's father put a hand on her arm and murmured that she was good to have come. 'I'm awfully sorry, Robert,' she said again, murmuring also.

She knew him as Connie's father, her own daughter, Melissa, being Connie's particular friend. She didn't know him well; more often than not he wasn't there when she brought Melissa to spend the day at the farm. She had liked Connie's mother but had never had much of a conversation with her, they being different kinds of people, and the house was a busy place. During all the years Teresa had known the house no one was employed to help in it, as no one was – except for odd days during the summer – on the farm itself. Teresa had guessed that the present bleak occasion would be in the hands of Mrs O'Daly, who in her capable countrywoman's way would have offered to see to things. She poured the tea now, cups and saucers laid out on a table that didn't belong in the drawing-room. O'Daly, a small, scuttling man who worked on the roads and took on anything else he could get, was handing round plates of biscuits and egg sandwiches.

'He did it very well,' someone remarked to Teresa. 'Your rector did.'

'Yes, he did.'

A couple she couldn't place, whose way of referring to Mr Crozier suggested they weren't of the locality, nodded a nervous confirmation of her agreement. Teresa thought she probably would even have known them if they'd come out from Clonmel. Yes, Mr Crozier did funerals well, she said.

'We're distant cousins,' the woman said. 'A generation back.'

'I live quite near.'

'It's lovely here.'

'Quiet,' the man said. 'You'd notice the quiet.'

'We didn't know until we picked up the *Irish Times*,' the woman said. 'Well, we'd lost touch.'

'Saddens us now, of course.' The man nodded that into place. 'To have lost touch.'

'Yes.'

Teresa was forty-one, still pretty, her round face brightened by a smile that came easily and lingered, as if it belonged to these features in a way as permanent as they were themselves. Her reddish hair was cut quite short; she had to watch her weight and adamantly did so. She shook her head when O'Daly pressed his plate of Bourbon creams on her.

'We drove over,' the woman she was in conversation with imparted. 'From Mitchelstown.'

'Good of you to come.'

They deprecated that, and Teresa looked around. When she woke that morning she'd found herself wondering if her husband would be here, if he'd drive down from Dublin, since the death would have shocked him. But among the mourners in the drawing-room she didn't see him. It seemed quite a sparse attendance in the large, ordinarily furnished room, for not everyone who'd been at the church had come. But Teresa knew her husband hadn't been in the church either. It was years now since they'd met; he'd ceased to bother with his children as soon as other children were born to him. As good as his word about not being a nuisance, Teresa supposed.

\*

Afterwards, when everyone had gone, Connie helped the O'Dalys to clear up and when that was done the O'Dalys went too. She and her father did what her mother had requested then, taking her things from the wardrobe and the dressing-table drawers, disposing of them as she had wished, her charities remembered. It was late before all that was completed, before Connie and her father sat together in the kitchen. He poached their eggs when they'd decided to have eggs. He asked her to watch the toast. 'We'll manage,' he said.

*

The farm had come to Robert when he married, introducing him to a way of life he had not sought and which he did not imagine he would take to. In fact, he did, and over the years transformed the farm his wife had not long ago inherited as a sluggish, neglected enterprise into a fairly thriving one. It was a means of livelihood too; and, more than that, a source of personal satisfaction for Robert that he succeeded with crops and stock, about which he had once known nothing.

All this continued when he was widowed, when the house and land became entirely his. There were no changes on the farm, but in the house – to which Mrs O'Daly now came for three hours every weekday morning – Connie and her father, while slowly coming to terms with the loss they had suffered, shared the awareness of a ghost that fleetingly demanded no more than to be remembered. Life continuing could not fold away what had happened but it offered something, blurring the drama of death's immediacy. And then, when almost two years had passed since the funeral, Robert asked Teresa to marry him.

It was a natural thing. Having known one another through the friendship of their daughters, they had come to know one another better in the new circumstances, Teresa continuing to drive Melissa to the farm, with her much younger brother when he was made welcome there by Connie but was still too young to cycle. And Robert, doing his bit as often as he could, drove the two back to the bungalow at Fara Bridge, where their father in his day had attempted to get a pottery going.

The day he asked Teresa to marry him, Robert had looked up from the mangels he was weeding and seen her coming towards him, along the verge of the field. She brought him tea in a can, which she often did when she stayed all afternoon in order to save him the journey later to Fara Bridge. A year after the death she had begun to fall in love with him.

'I never knew,' he said in the mangel field when Teresa's response to his proposal was to tell him that. 'I thought you'd turn me down.'

She took the can of tea from his hand and lifted it to her lips, the first intimacy between them, before their first embrace, before they spoke of love. 'Oh, Robert, not in a million years would I turn you down,' she whispered.

There were difficulties, but they didn't matter as they would have once. In an Ireland they could both remember it would have been commented upon that she, born into a religious faith that was not Robert's, had attended a funeral service in his alien church. It would have been declared that marriage would not do; that the divorce which had brought Teresa's to an end could not be recognized. Questions would have been asked about children who might be born to them: to which belief were they promised, in which safe haven might they know only their own kind? Such difficulties still trailed, like husks caught in old cobwebs, but there were fewer interfering strictures now in how children were brought up, and havens were less often sought. Melissa, a year older than Connie, had received her early schooling from the nuns in Clonmel and had gone on to an undenominational boarding-school in Dublin. Her brother still attended the national school at Fara Bridge. Connie went to Miss Mortimer, whose tiny academy for Protestant children – her mother's choice because it was convenient – was conducted in an upstairs room at the rectory, ten minutes' away along the river path. But, in the end, all three would be together at Melissa's boarding-school, co-educational and of the present.

'How lovely all that is!' Teresa murmured.

*

There was a party at which the engagement was announced – wine in the afternoon, and Mrs O'Daly's egg sandwiches again, and Teresa's sponge cakes and her brandy-snaps and meringues. The sun came out after what had been a showery morning, allowing the celebration to take place in the garden. Overgrown and wild in places, the garden's neglect went back to the time of the death, although sometimes when she'd come to keep an eye on the children Teresa had done her best with the geranium beds, which had particularly been the task of Connie's mother.

She would do better now, Teresa promised herself, looking about among the guests as she had among the mourners, again half expecting to see the man who had left her, wanting him to be there, wanting him to know that she was loved again, that she had survived the indignity he had so casually subjected her to, that she was happy. But he wasn't there, as naturally he wouldn't be. All that was over, and the cousins from Mitchelstown with whom she had conversed on the afternoon of the funeral naturally weren't there either.

Robert was happy too – because Teresa was and because, all around him at the party, there were no signs of disapproval, only smiles of approbation.

*

Because the wedding was not to take place until later in the summer, after Melissa's return for the holidays, Connie and her father continued for a while to be alone together, managing, as he had said they would. Robert bought half a dozen Charollais calves, a breed he had never had on the farm before. He liked, every year, doing something new; and he liked the calves. Otherwise, his buying and selling were a pattern, his tasks a repetition.

He repaired the fences, tightening the barbed wire where that was possible, renewing it when it wasn't. He looked out for the many ailments that beset sheep. He lifted the first potatoes and noted every day the ripening of his barley.

Teresa dragged clumps of scotch grass and treacherous little nettles out of the sanguineum and the sylvaticum, taking a trowel to the docks. She cut down the Johnson's Blue, wary of letting it spread too wildly, but wouldn't have known to leave the Kashmir Purple a little longer, or that *pratense*'s sturdy roots were a job to divide. A notebook left behind instructed her in all that.

*

Miss Mortimer closed her small school for the summer and Connie was at home all day then. Sometimes Melissa's brother was there, a small thin child called Nat, a name that according to Melissa couldn't be more suitable, since he so closely resembled an insect.

'You want to come with us?' Teresa invited Connie when Melissa's term had ended and Teresa was setting off to meet her at the railway station in Clonmel. Connie hesitated, then said she didn't.

That surprised Teresa. She had driven over specially from Fara Bridge, as she always did when Melissa came back for the holidays. It surprised her, but afterwards she realized she'd somehow sensed before she spoke that Connie was going to say no. She was puzzled, but didn't let it show.

'Come back here, shall we?' she suggested, since this, too, was what always happened on Melissa's first evening home.

'If that's what you'd like,' Connie said.

The train was twenty minutes late and when Teresa returned to the farm with Melissa and Nat, Connie wasn't in the house, and when her father came in later she wasn't with him either, as she sometimes was. 'Connie!' they all called in the yard, her father going into some of the sheds. Melissa and her brother went to the end of the avenue and a little way along the road in both directions. 'Connie!' they called out in the garden, although they could see she wasn't there. 'Connie!' they called, going from room to room in the house. Her father was worried. He didn't say he was but Melissa and her brother could tell. So could Teresa.

'She can't be far,' she said. 'Her bicycle's here.'

She drove Melissa to Fara Bridge to unpack her things, and Nat went with them. She telephoned the farm then. There wasn't any answer and she guessed that Robert was still looking for his child.

\*

The telephone was ringing again when Connie came back. She came downstairs: she'd been on the roof, she said. You went up through the trapdoor at the top of the attic stairs. You could lie down on the warm lead and read a book. Her father shook his head, saying it wasn't safe to climb about on the roof. He made her promise not to again.

'What's the matter, Connie?' he asked her when he went to say goodnight. Connie said nothing was. Propped up in front of her was the book she'd been reading on the roof, *The Citadel* by A. J. Cronin.

'Surely you don't understand that, Connie?' her father said, and she said she wouldn't want to read a book she didn't understand.

\*

Connie watched the furniture being unloaded. The men lifted it from the yellow removal van, each piece familiar to her from days spent in the bungalow at Fara Bridge. Space had been made, some of the existing furniture moved out, to be stored in one of the outhouses.

Melissa wasn't there. She was helping her mother to rearrange in the half-empty rooms at Fara Bridge the furniture that remained, which would have to be sold when the bungalow was because there wasn't room for it at the farm. There had been a notice up all summer announcing the sale of the bungalow, but no one had made an offer yet. 'Every penny'll go into the farm,' Connie had heard Teresa saying.

Nat, whom Teresa had driven over earlier, watched with Connie in the hall. He was silent this morning, as he often was, his thin arms wrapped tightly around his body in a way that suggested he suffered from the cold, although the day was warm. Now and again he glanced at Connie, as if expecting her to say something about what was happening, but Connie didn't.

All morning it took. Mrs O'Daly brought the men tea and later, when they finished, Connie's father gave them a drink in the kitchen: small glasses of whiskey, except for the man who was the driver, who was given what remained in the bottle to take away with him.

'That's a lovely piece of delft,' Mrs O'Daly commented in the hall, referring to a blue-and-white soup tureen that the men had placed on the shelf of the hallstand. Having finished her morning's work, she had gone from room to room, inspecting the furniture that had come, and the glass and china in the hall. 'Isn't that really lovely!' she exclaimed again about the soup tureen.

It was cracked, Connie saw, a long crack in the lid. It used to be on the sideboard of the dining-room in the bungalow. She'd never much noticed it then, but in the hall it seemed obtrusive.

\*

Melissa was pretty, tall and slender, with long fair hair and greenish eyes. She liked jokes, and was clever although she didn't want to be and often pretended she wasn't.

'Time to measure the maggot,' she said later that same day. Her contention was that her brother had ceased to grow and would grow no more. She and Connie regularly made him stand against the door jamb of Connie's bedroom in the hope of finding an increase in his modest stature.

But Connie shook her head when this was again suggested. She was reading *London Belongs to Me* and went on doing so. Nat, on his way upstairs already, for he enjoyed this ceremonial attention, looked disappointed.

'Poor little maggot,' Melissa said. 'Poor little maggot, Connie. You've gone and upset it.'

'You shouldn't call your brother a maggot.'

'Hey!' Outraged, Melissa stared disbelievingly at Connie's calm features. 'Hey, come on!'

Connie turned down the corner of a page and began to walk away.

'It's only a blooming word,' Melissa ran after her to protest. 'He doesn't mind.'

'This isn't your house,' Connie said.

*

The day Connie's mother came back from the hospice Miss Mortimer had pinned up pictures of flowers. Miss Mortimer painted her pictures herself; before the flowers there'd been clowns. 'Foxglove,' Connie had said when Miss Mortimer asked.

Going home on the river path, she'd been thinking of that, of the four new pictures on the schoolroom wall, of Miss Mortimer saying that soon there wouldn't be a cowslip left anywhere. The schoolroom stayed on in her mind nearly always when she was going home, the writing on the blackboard, the tattered carpet, the boards showing all around it, the table they sat at, Miss Mortimer too. The rectory itself stayed in her mind, the two flights of stairs, the white hall door, three steps, the gravel.

Her father didn't wave when she saw him coming

towards her. It was drizzling and she thought that was maybe why he was coming to meet her. But often in winter it rained and he didn't; it was her mother who used to. 'Hullo, Connie,' he said, and she knew then that her mother had come back from the hospice, as she had said she would.

He took her hand, not telling her because she knew. She didn't cry. She wanted to ask in case it was different from what she guessed, but she didn't because she didn't want to hear if it was. 'It's all right,' her father said. He went with her to the room that had become her mother's, overlooking the garden. She touched her mother's hand and he lifted her up so that she could kiss her cheek, as often he'd done before. Mr Crozier was standing by the windows in the drawing-room when they went downstairs again. She hadn't known he was there. Then the O'Dalys came.

'You stay here with me,' Mrs O'Daly said in the kitchen. 'I'll hear you your reading.' But it wasn't reading on a Tuesday, another verse to learn instead, and six sentences to write. 'You going to write them then?' Mrs O'Daly asked. 'You going to think them up?'

She didn't want to. She learned the verse and said it to her father when he came to sit beside her, but the next day she didn't have to go to Miss Mortimer's. People came in the morning. She could hear their footsteps in the hall and on the stairs; she couldn't hear voices. It was in the afternoon that her mother died.

\*

'That's not like Connie,' Robert said.

'No, it isn't.'

When Teresa had been told by her children what Connie had said to them she had guessed, with sudden, bitter intuition, that everything going well was over. And she had wondered where she and Robert had gone wrong. Robert was simply bewildered.

The wedding – to be conducted by Mr Crozier as a purely family occasion – was less than three weeks off. No going away afterwards, no honeymoon because the time of year on the farm wasn't right for that.

'What else does Connie say?'

Teresa shook her head. She didn't know but suspected nothing else, and was right.

'We want to be married,' Robert said. 'Nothing's going to stop that now.'

Teresa hesitated, but only for a moment. 'Nothing is,' she said.

'Children manage to get on. Even when they're strangers to one another.'

Teresa didn't say that being strangers might make things easier. She didn't say it because she didn't know why that should be. But Melissa, who never wept, wept often now, affected as a stranger would not have been.

\*

The books Connie pretended to read were in the dining-room bookcases, on either side of the fireplace. They'd been her mother's books, picked up at country-house auctions, some thrown away when the shelves became full, all of them old, belonging to another time. '*The Man with Red Hair*,' her mother said, 'you'll love that.' And *Dr Bradley Remembers*, and *Random Harvest*. Only *Jamaica Inn* retained its paper jacket, yellow, without a picture. 'And *The Stars Look Down*,' her mother had said. 'You'll love *The Stars Look Down*.'

Connie took it to the roof, to the lead-covered gully she had found, wide enough to lie on between two slopes of slates. Every time she went there she wished she didn't have to disobey her father and always took care not to spend too long there in case she was discovered. Sometimes she stood up, protected from sight by the bulk of a chimney and, far away, saw her father in the fields or Teresa among the geraniums. Sometimes Melissa and Nat were on the avenue, Nat on the carrier of Melissa's bicycle, his small legs spread wide so that they wouldn't catch in the spokes.

\*

Teresa felt she had never loved Robert more; and felt that she was loved, herself, more steadfastly even than before – as if, she thought, the trouble brought such closeness. Or was there panic? she wondered in other moments; was it in panic that the depths of trust were tapped? Was it in panic that the widowed and the rejected protected what they'd been unable to protect before? She did not know the answers to her questions. It only seemed all wrong that a child's obduracy should mock what was so fairly due.

\*

'Connie.'

Robert found her in the outhouse where the furniture was. She had folded aside a dust-sheet and was sitting in an armchair of which the springs had gone, which should have been thrown out years ago.

'Connie,' he interrupted her, for she had not heard him. Her book was *Folly Bridge*.

She marked her place with a finger. She smiled at him. No one considered that recently she'd turned sulky; there was no sign of that. Even when she'd told Melissa and Nat that the house was not theirs, she had apparently simply said it.

'You're troubled because Teresa and I are to be married, Connie.'

'I'm all right.'

'You didn't seem to mind before.'

The armchair had a high back with wings, its faded red velvet badly worn in places, an embroidery of flowers stitched into where an antimacassar might be.

'It's very good,' Connie said, speaking about the book she held.

'Yes.'

'Will you read it?'

'If you would like me to.'

Connie nodded. And they could talk about it, she said. If he read it they could talk about it.

'Yes, we could. You've always liked Teresa, Connie. You've always liked Melissa and Nat. It isn't easy for us to understand.'

'Couldn't it stay here, the furniture you don't want? Couldn't we keep it here?'

'Out here it's a bit damp for furniture.'

'Couldn't we put it back then?'

'Is that what's worrying you, Connie? The furniture?'

'When the books are thrown away I'll know what every single one of them was about.'

'But, for heaven's sake, the books won't be thrown away!'

'I think they will be, really.'

Robert went away. He didn't look for Teresa to tell her about the conversation. Every year at this time he erected a corral where his ewes paddled through a trough of disinfectant. They crowded it now, while he remembered his half-hearted protestations and Connie's unsatisfactory responses. 'Oh, come on, come on! Get on with it!' Impatient with his sheep, as he had not been with his daughter, he wondered if Connie hated him. He had felt she did, although nothing like it had showed, or had echoed in her voice.

\*

From the roof she saw a car she'd never seen before, and guessed why it had come. In one of the drawers of the rickety Welsh dresser she'd found a shopping list and thought she remembered its being lost. *Ironing starch. Baking powder*, she'd read.

The car that had come was parked in the yard when she came down from the roof. A man was standing beside it. He referred to the furniture that was to be sold, as Connie had thought he might.

'Anyone around?' he asked her.

He was a big red-faced man in shirtsleeves. He'd thought he'd never find the house, he said. He asked her if he was expected, if this was the right place, and she wanted to say it wasn't, but Teresa came out of the house then.

'Go and get your father,' she said, and Connie nodded and went to where she'd seen him from the roof.

'Don't sell the furniture,' she begged instead of saying the man had come.

\*

One night, when the wedding was five days away, Teresa drove over to the farm. About to go to bed, she knew she wouldn't be able to sleep and wrote a note for Melissa, saying where she was going. It was after half past one and if there hadn't been a sign of life at the farm she would have driven away again. But the lights were on in the big drawing-room and Robert heard the car. He'd been drinking, he confessed as he let Teresa in.

'I don't know how to make sense to her,' he said when they'd embraced. Without asking, he poured her some whiskey. 'I don't know what to do, Teresa.'

'I know you don't.'

'When she came to stand beside me while I was milking this afternoon, when she didn't say anything but I could hear her pleading, I thought she was possessed. But later on we talked as if none of all this was happening. She laid the table. We ate the trout I'd fried. We washed the plates up. Dear Teresa, I can't destroy the childhood that is left to her.'

'I think you're perhaps a little drunk.'

'Yes.'

He did not insist that there must be a way; and knowing what frightened him, Teresa knew there wasn't. She was frightened herself while she was with him now, while wordlessly they shared the horrors of his alarm. Was some act, too terrible for a child, waiting in the desolation of despair to become a child's? They did not speak of what imagination made of it, how it might be, nurtured in anger's pain, in desperation and betrayal, the ways it might become unbearable.

They walked on the avenue, close to one another in the refreshing air. The sky was lightening, dawn an hour away. The shadows of danger went with them, too treacherous to make chances with.

'Our love still matters,' Teresa whispered. 'It always will.'

★

A calf had been born and safely delivered. It had exhausted him: Connie could tell her father was tired. And rain that had begun a week ago had hardly ceased, washing his winter seeding into a mire.

'Oh, it'll be all right,' he said.

He knew what she was thinking, and he watched her being careful with the plates that were warming in the oven, careful with the coffee she made, letting it sit a moment. Coffee at suppertime was what he'd always liked. She heated milk and poured it from the saucepan.

The bread was sawn, slices waiting on the board, butter beside them. There were tomatoes, the first of the Blenheims, the last of the tayberries. Pork steak browned on the pan.

It was not all bleakness: Robert was aware of that. In moments like the moments that were passing now, and often too at other times, he discerned in what had been his daughter's obduracy a spirit, still there, that was not malicious. In the kitchen that was so familiar to both of them, and outside in the raw cold of autumn when she came to him in the fields, she was as events had made her, the recipient of a duty she could not repudiate. It had seemed to her that an artificial household would demand that she should, and perhaps it might have.

Robert had come to understand that; Teresa confessed that nothing was as tidy as she'd imagined. There were no rights that cancelled other rights, less comfort than she'd thought for the rejected and the widowed, no fairness either. They had been hasty, she dared to say, although two years might seem a long enough delay. They had been clumsy and had not known it. They had been careless, yet were not careless people. They were a little to blame, but only that.

And Robert knew that time in passing would settle how the summer had been left. Time would gather up the ends, and see to it that his daughter's honouring of a memory was love that mattered also, and even mattered more.

# Old Flame

*Grace died.*

As Zoë replaces the lid of the electric kettle – having steamed the envelope open – her eye is caught by that stark statement. As she unfolds the plain white writing-paper, another random remark registers before she begins to read from the beginning. *We never quarrelled not once that I remember.*

The spidery scrawl, that economy with punctuation, were once drooled over by her husband, and to this day are not received in any ordinary manner, as a newspaper bill is, or a rates demand. Because of the sexual passion there has been, the scrawl connects with Charles's own neat script, two parts of a conjunction in which letters have played an emotional part. Being given to promptness in such matters, Charles will at once compose a reply, considerate of an old flame's due. Zoë feared this correspondence once, and hated it. *As ever my love, Audrey*: in all the years of the relationship the final words have been the same.

As always, she'll have to reseal the envelope because the adhesive on the flap has lost its efficacy. Much easier all that is nowadays, with convenient sticks of Pritt or Uhu. Once, at the height of the affair, she'd got glue all over the letter itself.

Zoë, now seventy-four, is a small, slender woman, only a little bent. Her straight hair, once jet-black, is almost white. What she herself thinks of as a letterbox mouth caused her, earlier in her life, to be designated attractive rather than beautiful. 'Wild' she was called as a girl, and 'unpredictable', both terms relating to her temperament. No one has ever called her pretty, and no one would call her wild or unpredictable now.

Because it's early in the day she is still in her dressing-gown, a pattern of tulips in black-and-scarlet silk. It hugs her slight body, crossed over on itself in front, tied with a matching sash. When her husband appears he'll still be in his dressing-gown also, comfortably woollen, teddy-bear brown stitched with braid. *Dearest, dearest Charles*, the letter begins. Zoë reads all of it again.

This letter is special, of course, because of Grace's death. Others have been different. *Grace and I wondered how you are getting along these days . . . Grace and I have finally taken retirement . . . I'm to give you this address Grace says. Just in case you ever want to write . . . A seaside house. Grace always wanted that . . .* In 1985, in 1978 and '73 and '69, Grace always had a kind of say. *A quick lunch some time?* each letter – this one too – suggests before the *As ever my love* and the single cross that's a reminder of their kissing. Somehow, Zoë has always believed, the quick-lunch suggestion came from Grace. Did she, she wonders, make it again on her deathbed?

The affair has developed in Zoë an extra sense. Without making an effort she can visualize a tall woman she has never met, now the lone occupant of a house she has never entered. She sees her smartly dressed in shades of maroon, iron-grey hair fashionably arranged, the clarity of her eyes a little clouded. Creases have multiplied on the skin of her face and are a map of wrinkles now. Zoë imagines her entering her kitchen and turning on the radio, to hear the same news she herself heard earlier: football fans on the rampage in a German city, shop windows smashed, a bus turned on its side. She imagines her standing with a cup of Nescafé in the bow-window of her sitting-room: seen through drizzle on a pane, the sea is a pattern of undulations, greyish green, scuffed with white. The sky that meets it on the far horizon is too dull to contemplate. A single mackerel-trawler slips into view.

*If it's inconvenient or if you'd rather not well of course I understand.*

The Alp Horn is where they lunch, have done so since first they loved one another. Her inquisitiveness getting the better of her, Zoë went there once. She actually went inside, giving a name she had made up, of someone she was to meet there. A musical instrument, presumably an alp horn, stretched the length of a wall; Tyrolean landscape decorated two others. There were checked tablecloths, blue and red; recorded music played; the place was modest. 'I'm awfully sorry,' Zoë said to a waiter, half a lifetime ago it seems like because in fact it is. 'Clearly there's been a muddle.'

She finds the Pritt where Charles keeps it, in the middle drawer of the dresser, with his writing things and sealing-wax, Sellotape and scissors. She boils the water in the kettle again, for coffee. She hears his footstep above her, crossing the landing from their bedroom to the lavatory, crossing it again to the bathroom. Pipes rattle when he turns on the hot water because he has never learned not to turn the tap all the way in order to prevent it gushing so. All the years she has known him he has been impatient about things like that.

'It's time you saw Charles again,' Zoë knows Grace used to say in that house, and guesses Audrey's reply: that Charles has his own life now, that Charles has made his choice. Grace always pressed, gently, because she loved Charles, too, but had to keep it to herself. 'My dear, I'm certain Charles would welcome a sign.' Anything could have happened: they'd never know.

Thirty-nine years have passed since the first year of the great passion. Audrey and Grace were friends already, making their way in office life, both of them determined to use their secretarial posts as stepping-stones to something better. The day Charles appeared – the first time they laid eyes on him – he was being led around by the snooty, half-drunk Miss Maybury, both of them with glasses of *vin rosé*, which was what La Maybury – her office title – drank every afternoon, sometimes in the mornings also. 'Hullo,' Charles said, a lanky young man with floppy fair hair. It wasn't difficult for Zoë to imagine the shy smile he'd darted at Audrey and then at Grace. Afterwards he'd told her about La Maybury and the wine and the tour round the office.

'Poor Charles' he had become in after years. Poor Charles alone with his unloved, unloving wife. What was the point of any of it, now that his children were grown-up? In their seaside house they lived in hope – that one day he would sound less whispery on the telephone, passing on details of death by misadventure or disease. 'Given six months, a merciful release.' Or: 'Just slipped. A wretched plastic bag. In the rain, near the dustbins.'

Zoë places two slices of bread in the toaster but does not press the lever down because it isn't time to yet. Before the affair got going it had been a subject of fascination to him that two such apparently close friends should, in appearance at least, be so vastly different. 'Oh, that's often so,' Zoë said, citing examples from her schooldays, but he had never shown much interest in her schooldays and he didn't then. 'Grace the lumpy one's called,' he said. 'Back of a bus. Audrey's the stunner.' Old-fashioned names, she had thought, and imagined old-fashioned girls, frumpish in spite of Audrey's looks. Later, he'd always included Grace in his references to Audrey, clouding the surface because of the depths beneath.

She measures coffee into a blue Denby pot, the last piece of a set. There was a photograph she found once: Audrey as handsome as he'd claimed, a goddess-like creature with a cigarette; Grace blurred, as if she'd moved. They were sprawled on a rug beside a tablecloth from which a picnic had been eaten. You could see part of the back wheel of a car, and it wasn't difficult to sharpen into focus Grace's frizzy hair, two pink-rimmed eyes behind her spectacles. Where on earth had that picnic been? What opportunity had been seized – a slack afternoon in the office?

Zoë props the letter against his cup, doing so with deliberation. It will vex him that she has arranged it so, the gesture attaching a comment of her own; but then she has been vexed herself. She tore that photograph into little pieces and watched them burn. He never mentioned its loss, as naturally he wouldn't.

'Ah, good,' she greets him, and watches while he picks the letter up. She depresses the lever of the toaster. The milk saucepan rattles on the gas, a glass disc bouncing about in it to prevent the milk from boiling over. She pours their coffee. He returns the letter to its envelope. She halves each piece of toast diagonally, the way he likes it.

She hadn't guessed. It was a frightening, numbing shock when he said: 'Look, I have to tell you. Audrey and I have fallen in love.' Just for a moment she couldn't think who Audrey was. 'Audrey and I,' he repeated, thinking she hadn't properly heard. 'Audrey and I love one another.' For what remained of that year and for several years following it, Zoë felt physically sick every time that statement echoed, coming back to her from its own Sunday morning: 10th September 1968, eleven o'clock. He had chosen the time because they'd have all day to go into things, yet apart from practicalities there was nothing to go into. They couldn't much go into the fact that he wanted someone else more than he wanted her. After five years of marriage he was tired of her. He had spoken in order to be rid of her.

Finishing with the marmalade, she moves it closer to him. His face, less expert at disguise than once it was, hides nothing. She watches him thinking about the woman who has been left on her own, his sympathy reaching into a seaside house that's now too spacious for one. But Charles is not an imaginative man. He doesn't penetrate far. He doesn't see in the old flame's fridge a chicken joint for one, and fish for one tomorrow. Winter's a melancholy time to be bereaved, a mood reflected in the cold and wet, winds rattling and whining. Audrey'll miss her friend particularly when it comes to watching television, no one beside her to share a comment with.

'Oh yes, the Alp Horn's still there,' Zoë hears a little later that morning, having eased open a door he has carefully closed. 'Twelve forty-five, should we say? If your train's a little late, anything like that, please don't worry. I'll simply wait, my dear.'

He'd been saying something she hadn't managed to hear before that, his voice unnaturally low, a hand cupped round the mouthpiece. Then there'd been the hint of a reprimand because the old flame hadn't written sooner. Had he known he'd have gone to the funeral.

'I'm sorry to have hurt you so,' he said later that Sunday, but words by then made no sense whatsoever. Five years of a mistake, she thought, two children mistakenly born. Her tears dripped on to her clothes while he stood there crestfallen, his good looks distorted by distress. She did not blow her nose; she wanted to look as she felt. 'You would like me dead,' she sobbed, willing him to raise his fist in fury at her, to crash it down on her, obliterating in mercy all that remained of her. But he only stood there, seeming suddenly ill-fed. Had she not cooked properly for him? her thoughts half crazily ran on. Had she not given him what was nourishing? 'I thought we were happy,' she whispered. 'I thought we didn't need to question anything.'

'Nice to see the old Alp Horn again,' his murmur comes from the hall, and Zoë can tell that he's endeavouring to be cheerful. 'Tell you what, I'll bring a packet of Three Castles.'

There is the click of the receiver, the brief sounding of the bell. He says something to himself, something like 'Poor thing!' Zoë softly closes the door. Grace and Audrey had probably been friends for fifty years, might even have been schoolfriends. Was Audrey the one whom other girls had pashes on? Was Grace a little bullied? Zoë imagines her hunched sulkily into a desk, and Audrey standing up for her. In letters and telephone conversations there have been references to friends, to holidays in Normandy and Brittany, to bridge, to Grace's colonic irrigation, to Audrey's wisdom teeth removed in hospital. Zoë knows – she doesn't often call it guessing – that after Audrey's return from every visit to the Alp Horn Grace was greedy for the morsels passed on to her. Not by the blink of an eye could Grace reveal her secret; the only expression of her passion was her constancy in urging another letter. *We think of you with her in that coldness.* 'Quite frail he looked,' Audrey no doubt reported in recent years.

He did not stay with Zoë in 1967 because of love. He stayed because – quite suddenly, and unexpectedly – the emotions all around him seemed to have become too much: it was weariness that caused him to back off. Had he sensed, Zoë wondered years later, the shadow of Grace without entirely knowing that that was what it was? He stayed, he said, because Zoë and the two children who had then been born meant more than he had estimated. Beneath this statement there was the implication that for the sake of his own happiness it wasn't fair to impose hardship on the innocent. That, though unspoken, had a bitter ring for Zoë. 'Oh, go away!' she cried. 'Go to that unpleasant woman.' But she did not insist; she did not say there was nothing left, that the damage had been done for ever. To the woman, he quoted his economic circumstances as the reason for thinking again. Supporting two households – which in those days was what the prospect looked like – was more than daunting. *Grace says you wouldn't have to leave them penniless. What she and I earn could easily make up for that. Grace would love to help us out.* Had he gone, Grace would somehow have been there too.

*

Zoë knows when the day arrives. Glancing across their breakfast coffee at her, his eyes have a dull sparkle that's caused by an attempt to rekindle an obsolete excitement: he was always one to make an effort. In a letter once Audrey referred to his 'loose-limbed charm', stating that she doubted she could live without it and be herself. He still has that lanky look, which perhaps was what she meant; what remains of his floppy fair hair, mainly at the back and sides of his head, is ash-coloured now; his hands – which Zoë can well imagine either Grace or Audrey designating his most elegant feature – have a shrivelled look, the bones more pronounced than once they were, splotches of freckles on skin like old paper. His face is beakier than it was, the teeth for the most part false, his eyes given to watering when a room is warm. Two spots of pink come and go high up on his narrow cheeks, where the structure of the cheekbones tautens the skin. Otherwise, his face is pale.

'I have to go in today,' he casually announces.

'Not here for lunch?'

'I'll pick up a sandwich somewhere.'

She would like to be able to suggest he'd be wiser to go to a more expensive restaurant than the Alp Horn. Cheap food and house wine are a deadly combination at his time of life. A dreadful nuisance it is when his stomach goes wrong.

'Bit of shopping to do,' he says.

Once there was old so-and-so to meet but that doesn't work any more because, with age, such figures can't be counted upon not to give the game away. There was 'the man at Lloyd's' to see, or Hanson and Phillips, who were arranging an annuity. All that has been tapped too often: what's left is the feebleness of shopping. Before his retirement there was no need to mention anything at all.

'Shopping,' she says without an interrogative note. 'Shopping.'

'One or two things.'

Three Castles cigarettes are difficult to find. Audrey will smoke nothing else and it's half a joke that he goes in search of them, a fragment of affection in the kaleidoscope of the love affair. Another such fragment is their shared delight in sweetbreads, a food Zoë finds repellent. They share unpunctuality also. *Grace can't understand how we ever manage to meet!*

'Should keep fine,' he predicts.

'Take your umbrella all the same.'

'Yes, I'll take my umbrella.'

He asks about a particular shirt, his blue striped one. He wonders if it has been ironed. She tells him where it is. Their three children – the boys, and Cecilia, born later, all married now – know nothing about Audrey. Sometimes it seems odd to Zoë that this should be so, that a person who has featured so profoundly in their father's life should be unknown to them. If that person had had her way Cecilia would not have been born at all.

'Anything you need?' he offers. 'Anything I can get you?'

She shakes her head. She wishes she could say: 'I open her letters. I listen when there's a phone conversation.' She wishes he could tell her that Grace has died, that his friend is now alone.

'Back about four, I expect?'

'Something like that.'

Had he gone off, she wouldn't still be in this house. She wouldn't be sitting in this kitchen in her black-and-scarlet dressing-gown, eyeing him in his woolly brown one. She'd be living with one of the children or in a flat somewhere. Years ago the house would have been sold; she'd not have grown old with a companion. It was most unlikely there would ever have been another man; she doubted she'd have wanted one.

'I dreamed we were on a ferry going to Denmark,' he unexpectedly says. 'There was a woman you got talking to, all in black.'

'Prettily in black?'

'Oh, yes. A pretty woman too. She used an odd expression. She said she was determined to have what she called a "corking child".'

'Ah.'

'You sat me down in front of her and made me comment on her dress. You made me make suggestions.'

'And did you, Charles?'

'I did. I suggested shades of green. Deep greens; not olive like my trousers. And rounded collar-ends on her shirt, not pointed like mine. I made her look at mine. She was a nice woman except that she said something a little rude about my shoes.'

'Scuffed?'

'Something like that.'

'Your shoes are never scuffed.'

'No.'

'Well, there you are.'

He nods. 'Yes, there you are.'

Soon after that he rises and goes upstairs again. Why did that conversation about a dream take place? It's true that just occasionally they tell one another their dreams; just occasionally, they have always done so. But significance appears to attach to the fact that he shared his with her this morning: that is a feeling she has.

'Why did you bother with me if I didn't matter?' Long after he'd decided to stay with her she asked him that. Long afterwards she questioned everything; she tore at the love that had united them in the first place; it was her right that he should listen to her. Six years went by before their daughter was born.

'Well, I'm off.'

Like a tall, thin child he looks, his eyes deep in their sockets, his dark, conventional suit well pressed, a Paisley tie in swirls of blue that matches the striped blue shirt. His brown shoes, the pair he keeps for special occasions, gleam as they did not in his eccentric dream.

'If I'd known I'd have come with you.' Zoë can't help saying that; she doesn't intend to, the words come out. But they don't alarm him, as once they would have. Once, a shadow of terror would have passed through his features, apprehension spreading lest she rush upstairs to put her coat on.

'We'll go in together next time,' he promises.

'Yes, that'll be nice.'

They kiss, as they always do when they part. The hall door bangs behind him. She'll open a tin of salmon for lunch and have it with tomatoes and a packet of crisps. A whole tin will be too much, of course, but between them they'll probably be able for whatever's left this evening.

In the sitting-room she turns the television on. Celeste Holm, lavishly fur-coated, is in a car, cross about something. Zoë doesn't want to watch and turns it off again. She imagines the old flame excited as the train approaches London. An hour ago the old flame made her face up, but now she does it all over again, difficult with the movement of the train. Audrey doesn't know that love came back into the marriage, that skin grew over the wound. She doesn't know, because no one told her, because he cannot bring himself to say that the brief occasion was an aberration. He honours – because he's made like that – whatever it is the affair still means to the woman whose life it has disrupted. He doesn't know that Audrey – in receipt of all that was on offer – would have recovered from the drama in a natural way if Grace – in receipt of nothing at all – hadn't been an influence. He doesn't wonder what will happen now, since death has altered the pattern of loose ends.

Opening the salmon tin, Zoë travels again to the Alp Horn rendezvous. She wonders if it has changed and considers it unlikely. The long horn still stretches over a single wall. The same Tyrolean landscape decorates two others. There are the blue-and-red tablecloths. He waits with a glass of sherry, and then she's there.

'My dear!'

She is the first to issue their familiar greeting, catching him unaware the way things sometimes do these days.

'My dear!' he says in turn.

Sherry is ordered for her, too, and when it comes the rims of their glasses touch for a moment, a toast to the past.

'Grace,' he says. 'I'm sorry.'

'Yes.'

'Is it awful?'

'I manage.'

The waiter briskly notes their order and enquires about the wine.

'Oh, the good old house red.'

Zoë's fingers, gripping and slicing a tomato, are arthritic, painful sometimes though not at present. In bed at night he's gentle when he reaches out for one hand or the other, cautious with affection, not tightening his grasp as once he did. Her fingers are ugly; she sometimes thinks she looks quite like a monkey now. She arranges the fish and the tomato on a plate and sprinkles pepper over both. Neither of them ever has salt.

'And you, Charles?'

'I'm all right.'

'I worry about you sometimes.'

'No, I'm all right.'

It was accordion music that was playing in the Alp Horn the day Zoë's inquisitiveness drove her into it. Young office people occupied the tables. Business was quite brisk.

'I do appreciate this,' Audrey says. 'When something's over, all these years – I do appreciate it, Charles.'

He passes across the table the packet of Three Castles cigarettes, and she smiles, placing it beside her because it's too soon yet to open it.

'You're fun, Charles.'

'I think La Maybury married, you know. I think someone told me that.'

'Grace could never stand her.'

'No.'

Is this the end? Zoë wonders. Is this the final fling, the final call on his integrity and honour? Can his guilt slip back into whatever recesses there are, safe at last from Grace's second-hand desire? No one told him that keeping faith could be as cruel as confessing faithlessness; only Grace might have appropriately done that, falsely playing a best friend's role. But it wasn't in Grace's interest to do so.

'Perhaps I'll sell the house.'

'I rather think you should.'

'Grace did suggest it once.'

Leaving them to it, Zoë eats her salmon and tomato. She watches the end of the old black-and-white film: years ago they saw it together, long before Grace and Audrey. They've seen it together since; as a boy he'd been in love with Bette Davis. Picking at the food she has prepared, Zoë is again amused by what has amused her before. But only part of her attention is absorbed. Conversations take place; she does not hear; what she sees are fingers undistorted by arthritis loosening the cellophane on the cigarette packet and twisting it into a butterfly. He orders coffee. The scent that came back on his clothes was lemony with a trace of lilac. In a letter there was a mention of the cellophane twisted into a butterfly.

'Well, there we are,' he says. 'It's been lovely to see you, Audrey.'

'Lovely for me too.'

When he has paid the bill they sit for just a moment longer. Then, in the ladies', she powders away the shine that heat and wine have induced, and tidies her tidy grey hair. The lemony scent refreshes, for a moment, the stale air of the cloakroom.

'Well, there we are, my dear,' he says again on the street. Has there ever, Zoë wonders, been snappishness between them? Is she the kind not to lose her temper, long-suffering and patient as well as being a favourite girl at school? After all, she never quarrelled with her friend.

'Yes, there we are, Charles.' She takes his arm. 'All this means the world to me, you know.'

They walk to the corner, looking for a taxi. Marriage is full of quarrels, Zoë reflects.

\*

'Being upright never helps. You just lie there. Drink lots of water, Charles.'

The jug of water, filled before she'd slipped in beside him last night, is on his bedside table, one glass poured out. Once, though quite a while ago now, he not only insisted on getting up when he had a stomach upset but actually worked in the garden. All day she'd watched him, filling his incinerator with leaves and weeding the rockery. Several times she'd rapped on the kitchen window, but he'd taken no notice. As a result he was laid up for a fortnight.

'I'm sorry to be a nuisance,' he says.

She smoothes the bedclothes on her side of the bed,

giving the bed up to him, making it pleasant for him in the hope that he'll remain in it. The newspaper is there for him when he feels like it. So is *Little Dorrit*, which he always reads when he's unwell.

'Perhaps consommé later on,' she says. 'And a cream cracker.'

'You're very good to me.'

'Oh, now.'

Downstairs Zoë lights the gas-fire in the sitting-room and looks to see if there's a morning film. *Barefoot in the Park* it is, about to begin. Quite suddenly then, without warning, she sees how the loose ends are. Everything is different, but nothing of course will ever be said. *So good the little restaurant's still there*, the old flame writes. *Just a line to thank you*. So good it was to talk. So good to see him. So good of him to remember the Three Castles. Yet none of it is any good at all because Grace is not there to say, 'Now tell me every single thing.' Not there to say when there's a nagging doubt, 'My dear, what perfect nonsense!' On her own in the seaside house she'll not find an excuse again to suggest a quick lunch if he'd like to. He'll not do so himself, since he never has. He'll gladly feel his duty done at last.

The old flame bores him now, with her scent and her cigarettes and her cellophane butterflies. In her seaside house she knows her thank-you letter is the last, and the sea is grey and again it rains. One day, on her own, she'll guess her friend was false. One day she'll guess a sense of honour kept pretence alive.

Grace died. That's all that happened, Zoë tells herself,

so why should she forgive? 'Why should I?' she murmurs. 'Why should I?' Yet for a moment before she turns on *Barefoot in the Park* tears sting her eyelids. A trick of old age, she tells herself, and orders them away.

# *Faith*

She was a difficult woman, had been a wilful child, a moody, recalcitrant girl given to flashes of temper; severity and suspicion came later. People didn't always know what they were doing, Hester liked to point out, readily speaking her mind, which she did most often to her brother, Bartholomew. She was forty-two now, he three years younger. She hadn't married, had never wanted to.

There was a history here: of Hester's influence while the two grew up together in crowded accommodation above a breadshop in a respectable Dublin neighbourhood. Their father was a clerk in Yarruth's timber yards, their mother took in sewing and crocheting. They were poor Protestants, modest behind trim net curtains in Maunder Street, pride taken in their religion, in being themselves. Her bounden duty, Hester called it, looking after Bartholomew.

When the time came, Bartholomew didn't marry either. An intense, serious young man, newly ordained into the Church of Ireland, he loved Sally Carbery and was accepted when he proposed. Necessarily a lengthy one, the engagement weathered the delay, but on the eve of the wedding it fell apart, which was a disappointment Bartholomew did not recover from. Sally Carbery – spirited and humorous, a source of strength during their friendship, beautiful in her way – married a man in Jacob's Biscuits.

Hester worked for the Gas Board, and gave that up to look after her father when he became a widower, suffering from Parkinson's disease for the last nine years of his life. That was her way; it was her nature, people said, compensation for her brusque manner; her sacrifice was applauded. 'We've always got on,' Hester said on the evening of their father's funeral. 'You and I have, Bartholomew.'

He didn't disagree, but knew that there was something missing in how his sister put this. They got on because, dutiful in turn, he saw to it that they did. Bartholomew's delicate good looks – fair hair, blue eyes – made the most of a family likeness that was less pleasing in Hester, his lithe ranginess cumbersome in a woman. All in all, it seemed only right that there should be adjustment, that any efforts made in the question of getting on should be his, and without acknowledgement.

Bartholomew didn't have a parish of his own. He assisted in one on the north side of the city, where Maunder Street was too: visiting the elderly, concerned with Youth Reach and Youth Action and the running of the Youth Centre, on Saturdays taking parties of children to ramble in the Dublin mountains or to swim in one of the northside's swimming-pools. He and Hester shared the family possessions when it was clearly no longer practical to retain the rented accommodation above the breadshop; Bartholomew found a room in the parish where he worked; Hester looked about for one. She made enquiries at the Gas Board about returning to a position similar to the one she had filled in the past, but for the moment there was nothing. Then she discovered Oscarey.

It was a townland in the Wicklow mountains, remote and bleak, once distinguished by the thriving presence of Oscarey House, of which no trace now remained. But the church that late in the house's existence had been built on the back avenue, for the convenience of the family and its followers, was still standing; and the estate's scattering of dwellings – the houndsman's and its yard and kennels, the gamekeeper's, the estate agent's pebble-dashed house – had undergone renovation and were all occupied. There was a Spar foodstore at Oscarey crossroads, an Esso petrol pump; letters could be posted a few miles away.

Bartholomew drove his sister to Oscarey when she asked him to. They went on a Monday, which was his free day, leaving early in the morning to avoid the Dublin traffic. He didn't know the purpose of their journey, hadn't yet been told, but Hester quite often didn't reveal her intentions, and he knew that eventually she would. It didn't occur to him to make the connection he might have.

'There's a man called Flewett,' Hester said in the car, reading the name from her own handwriting on a scrap of paper. 'He'll tell us.'

'What, though, Hester?'

She said then – a little, not much, not everything. The small church at Oscarey that had served a purpose in the past was being talked about again. A deprived Church of Ireland community, among it the descendants of indoor servants, gardeners and estate workers, was without a convenient means of worship. A consecrated building was mouldering through disuse.

They drove through Blessington, Bartholomew's very old A-30 van – used mainly for his Saturday trips to the mountains – making a tinny sound he hadn't noticed before. He didn't mention it but went on, hoping it was nothing much.

'It came to me,' Hester said.

'Who's Flewett, though?'

'One of the people around.'

She didn't say how she had heard about this man or offer further information about him.

'We'll see what Mr Flewett has to say,' she said.

Conversation with Hester was often like that; Bartholomew was used to it. Details withheld or frugally proffered made the most of what was imparted, as if to imbue communication with greater interest. Strangers sometimes assumed this to be so, only to realize a little later that Hester was not in the least concerned with such pandering: it was simply a quirk – without a purpose – that caused her to complicate conversation in this manner. She didn't know where it came from and did not ever wonder.

'What d'you think?' Bartholomew asked the man at the garage where he stopped for petrol, and the man said the tinny noise could be anything.

'Would you rev the engine for me?' he suggested,

opening the bonnet when he'd finished at the petrol pump. 'Give her the full throttle, sir,' he instructed, and then, 'D'you know what I'm going to tell you, sir? The old carburettor in this one's a bit shook. Ease her down now, sir, till we'll take a look.'

Bartholomew did so, then turned the engine off. As he understood it, the carburettor had loosened on its fixing. Adjusting a monkey wrench, the man said it would take two seconds to put right, and when it was done he wouldn't charge for it, although Bartholomew pressed him to.

'There was a line or two about Oscarey in the *Gazette*,' Hester said as they drove off again, referring to the magazine that was a source of Church of Ireland news. 'They're managing with a recorded service.'

It was as it always had been, she was thinking, Bartholomew offering the man money when it hadn't been asked for. The soft touch of the family, their father had called him, and used that same expression, laughing a bit, when Bartholomew first wanted to become a clergyman. But even so he hadn't been displeased; nor had their mother, nor Hester herself. Bartholomew's vocation suited him; it completed him, and protected him, as Hester tried to do in other ways.

'Lucky I called in there,' he was saying, and Hester sensed that he had guessed by now why they were driving to Oscarey. He had put it all together, which was why he referred again to the stop at the garage, for often he didn't want to talk about what had to be talked about, hoping that whatever it was would go away of its own accord. But this was something that shouldn't be allowed to go away, no matter how awkward and difficult it was.

'Good of him to want to help,' he said, and Hester watched a flight of rooks swirling out of a tree as they passed it.

'It's interesting, how things are,' she said. 'At Oscarey.'

It was still early when they arrived there, ten to eleven when Bartholomew drew up outside the Spar shop at the crossroads. 'A Mr Flewett?' he enquired at the single check-out, and was given directions.

He left the main road, drove slowly in a maze of lanes. Here and there there was a signpost. They found the church almost immediately after they turned into what had been the back avenue of Oscarey House, grown over now. There were graves but hardly what could be called a churchyard, no more than a narrow strip of land beside a path close to the church itself, running all the way round it. One of the graves, without a head-stone, was more recent than the others. The church was tiny, built of dark, almost black stone that gave it a forbidding air.

'A chapel of ease it might have been,' Bartholomew said.

'Mr Flewett'll know all about that.'

Inside, the church was musty, though with signs of use. The vases on the altar were empty, but there were hymn numbers – 8, 196, 516 – on the hymn board. The brass of the lectern was tarnished, and the brass of the memorial plates; the altarcloth was tattered and dingy. The slightly tinted glass of the windows – a bluish grey –

did not have biblical scenes. You couldn't call it much of a church, Bartholomew considered, but didn't say.

'It could be lovely,' his sister said.

*

Mr Flewett was elderly, which Hester had predicted he would be. He was on his own these days, he said, bringing tea on a tray, with biscuits in a tin. He had been welcoming at the hall door, although he had examined his visitors closely before he invited them into his house.

'We have the recording of the service, of course,' he said. 'I'm in charge of that myself. Morning prayer only.'

Oscarey Church was one of several in a combined benefice, the most distant being seventeen miles away. 'Too far for Canon Furney and there are a few who can't take to the recording so they make the journey to the canon at Clonbyre or Nead. On the other hand, of course, there's Mrs Wharton's kindness.'

That took some time to explain. The small scattered community of Oscarey was a mixture now of poor and better-off: besides the remnants of the estate families, there were newcomers. Mrs Wharton – no longer alive – had been one of the latter. Her will left her house and a considerable legacy to Oscarey Church, this money to provide a stipend for a suitable incumbent, the house to become Oscarey Rectory.

'That's what this is about,' Mr Flewett went on, pouring more tea.

Hester nodded. 'I heard something like it,' she said. 'That perhaps a younger man . . .'

'Indeed.'

Bartholomew felt uneasy. Hester often became carried away. In the sad, grimy little church he had understood how her imagination had been excited and still was; but the poverty of the place had a finality about it; even the attempts to disguise its neglect had. There was no obvious way in which the impossible could be reversed.

'The Church of Ireland moves slowly,' Mr Flewett said. 'I think we can agree about that. And of course Mrs Wharton died only five months ago. But time eats away at good intentions. Her wishes must be honoured. She is buried in our little graveyard.'

'I think we might have noticed,' Bartholomew said.

'Canon Furney is seventy-one. He'll not retire and there's no reason why he should. He's a good, dear man and no one would want him to. What we fear, though, is that when he goes, Clonbyre and Nead will be taken in with Oscarey again and Oscarey possibly abandoned, so far away we are. But Mrs Wharton's house would be a better rectory than the one there is now at Clonbyre, and her generosity otherwise is what the benefice is crying out for.'

'You've been very kind, Mr Flewett,' Bartholomew said. 'It's been interesting. But we've taken up your time and we mustn't do that.'

'Indeed you haven't. No, not at all.'

'I hope it all works out for you.'

'All of us at Oscarey hope that.'

Bartholomew stood up. He held out his hand, and then Mr Flewett shook Hester's hand too.

'I meant it in my letter,' he said. 'Come any time. I'm always here. People will be pleased you came.'

Hester nodded. She had a way sometimes of not smiling and she didn't now. But she nodded again as if to make up for that.

In the car Bartholomew said: 'What letter?'

Hester didn't answer. Preoccupied, she stared ahead. It was February, too soon for spring, but fine.

'Did you write to him, Hester?'

'The little piece in the *Gazette* was about that woman leaving money and the house. It gave his name.'

Bartholomew said nothing. His sister did things for the best: he'd always known that. It sometimes didn't seem so, but he knew it was.

'Will we have another look at the church?' she said.

He drew in when they came to it. The hump of earth they'd noticed, the newest of the graves, was just beginning to green over and had been tended, the grass clipped in a rectangle round it.

'I hope they know what they're doing,' Hester said, pushing open the heavy west door. 'I'd keep it locked myself.'

The missionary leaflets by the collection box were smeared and dog-eared, and Bartholomew noticed now that there was bird-lime on curtains that were there instead of a door to the vestry.

'I'd get rid of that coconut matting,' Hester said.

They didn't stop on the way back to Dublin. Hester

was quiet, as often she was, not saying anything until they were in Maunder Street. 'I have eggs I could scramble,' she said then, and Bartholomew followed her through the empty rooms.

'How long have you left here?' he asked, and his sister said until the end of next week. There'd been a place near Fairview Park and he asked about it. No good, she said, Drumcondra the same.

'I'm sorry you're having difficulties. I've kept an eye out.'

'The Gas Board'll have me back. Someone they weren't expecting to left.'

'Well, there's that at least.'

Hester was not enthusiastic. She didn't say, but Bartholomew knew. In the denuded kitchen he watched while she broke the yolks of the eggs with a fork, beating them up, adding milk and butter, then sprinkling on pepper. Since their childhood he had resented, without saying it, her interference, her indignation on his behalf, her possessiveness. He had forgiven what she couldn't help, doing so as natural in him as scorn and prickliness were in her. She had never noticed, had never been aware of how he felt.

'You'd take to Oscarey,' Hester said.

\*

Before Bartholomew and his sister made their lives at Oscarey, there was an inevitability about the course of events. In private, Bartholomew did not think about what was happening in terms of Hester, considering rather that this was what had been ordained for him, that Hester's ordering of the circumstances was part of that. Fifteen years ago, when Sally Carbery had decided against marriage at the last minute it was because she feared Hester. She had been vague when suddenly she was doubtful, and was less truthful than she might have been. Unaware of that at the time, Bartholomew was bewildered; later he came to believe that in influencing Sally Carbery's second thoughts Hester had, then too, been assigned a role in the pattern conceived by a greater wisdom. 'Silly', Hester's word for Sally Carbery had been, even before Sally Carbery and Bartholomew loved one another.

The Church approved the rescuing of Oscarey; and it was anticipated, as Mr Flewett had surmised, that when old Canon Furney died the benefice of Clonbyre, Nead and Oscarey would become one again, that the unnecessarily spacious, draughty rectory in poor repair at Clonbyre would be abandoned in favour of a smaller, more comfortable one at Oscarey. This came about, and the manner in which human existence – seeming to be shaped by the vagaries of time and chance but in fact obedient to a will – became the subject of more than one of Bartholomew's sermons. Verses of the scriptures were called upon to lend credence to his conclusions, which more than anything else claimed that the mysterious would never be less than mysterious, would always be there, at the heart of spiritual life. That the physical presence of things, and of words and people, amounted to very little made perfect sense to Bartholomew.

It did to Hester too. Belief was part of Hester, taken for granted, a sturdy certainty that brought her confidence and allowed her to insist she must be taken as she was, allowed her to condemn as a dishonesty any concealment of personal traits. When her brother's fourteen parishioners at Oscarey, and the twenty-seven at Clonbyre and the eleven at Nead, came to know her there was agreement – as elsewhere there had often been before – that she and Bartholomew were far from alike. None among the parishioners feared Hester as Sally Carbery had, since none possessed a fiancée's intuition, only strangers' perspicacity. Sally Carbery's fear – to do with the prospect of the future, of being more closely involved with Hester – was understandable. At Oscarey, and Clonbyre and Nead, there was only Hester as she was, a talking-point because of it.

As the two aged, the understanding between them that had survived the cramped conditions of Maunder Street was supported by reminiscence – the smell of fresh bread every early morning, the unexpected death of their mother, their father's mercilessly slow, the two cremations at Glasnevin. Seaside photographs taken at Rush and Bettystown were in an album, visits to both grandmothers and to aunts were remembered; and hearing other generations talked about were. The present was kept a little at bay: that congregations everywhere continued to dwindle, that no ground had been regained by the Church or seemed likely to be, was not often mentioned. Hester was indifferent to this. Bartholomew was increasingly a prey to melancholy, but did not let it show, to Hester or to anyone.

For her part, Hester had given herself the task of restoring Oscarey Church, scraping the tiled floor, washing the altarcloths, polishing the neglected pews and brass. The church was hers, she considered, for she had found it and brought life to it, making more of it than a mere outward and visible sign. It was not her way to say that all was well, that because of her work everything was good: there was a presumption in that she didn't care for, and such sentiments cloyed. But as she knelt before her brother at the altar-rails, while he raised the cup or again wiped clean its rim, she knew that all this was meant to be: he was here, where he should be, and so should she, where her unyielding spirit had brought them. 'The peace of God,' he ended each occasion of worship, and gave his blessing. The words were special. And her brother saying them in the hush while Hester still knelt among the few who came to Oscarey Church, before the shuffling and the whispering began, was special too.

Except at weddings and the christenings that sometimes followed them there were no young among the congregations of the three churches, and with nostalgia Bartholomew now and again remembered Youth Reach and Youth Action and the Saturday rambles to Kilmashogue and Two Rock. On Sundays when he looked down from the pulpit at aged faces, at tired eyes, heads turned to hear him better, and when his hand was afterwards shaken at the door, he sensed the hope that had flickered into life during the service: in all that was promised, in psalm and gospel, in his own interpretations, the end was not an end.

Then – as it happened, on a Sunday night – Bartholomew, with cruel suddenness, was aware of a realization that made him feel as if he had been struck a blow so powerful it left him, though not in pain, without the normality of his faculties. This happened in his bedroom before he had begun to undress. The bedside light was on; he had closed the door, pulled down the two blinds, and was standing beside his bed, having just untied the laces of his shoes. For a moment he thought he had fallen down, but he had not. He thought he could not see, but he could see. A shoe was in one hand, which brought something of reality back, and sitting down on the edge of the bed did too. The clatter of the shoe on the linoleum when it slipped from his grasp brought more. Sensations of confusion lingered while he sat there, then were gone.

'*Thy Kingdom come, Thy will be done on earth, As it is in heaven . . .*'

His own voice made no sense, and yet went on.

\*

Afterwards, Bartholomew told himself that what had occurred must surely be no more than a mood of petulance, an eruption from his half-stifled impatience with the embroidery and frills that dressed the simplicity of truth with invasive, sentimental stories that somehow made faith easier, the hymns he hated. For Bartholomew, the mystery that was the source of all spiritual belief, present through catastrophe and plague and evil, was a strength now too, and more than it had ever been. Yet there was disquiet, a stirring in his vocation he had brought upon himself and wished he had not. Seeking guidance, he dwelt on his memories of the euphoria he had been aware of when his profession had first seemed to be chosen for him. There were no reservations then, and he searched for what it was, in himself, that had allowed his unquestioning credence. But no help came from that far-off time, and Bartholomew − not knowing what he should otherwise do − continued to visit the lonely and the sick, to repeat the *Te Deum*, the Creed, the Litany. He felt he should not and yet he did.

*

Hester noticed no change in her brother, and he had told her nothing. Her own fulfilment, through him, continued, her belief undiminished, her certainties un-challenged. In her daily life all she distrusted she still distrusted. Her eye was cold, her scorn a nourishment; and then, for Hester too when more time passed, there was adversity. She did not complain. 'Oh, we all must die,' she said when she learned that she was to herself, sooner than she had ever expected. A doctor whom she had hardly bothered since coming to Oscarey confirmed his first suspicions, gently taking from her the small hope he had permitted to remain since her previous visit. He told her what she had to know, and she said nothing. Afterwards, alone, she did not weep; nor did she prepare her brother for what awaited both of them. But one morning, when the remains of spring and all of summer had gone, when they were sitting in warm September sunshine in their small garden, she told him. Hester was not yet sixty then.

*

Bartholomew listened with incredulous dismay. Yet Hester spoke so fearlessly, accepting as her due a simple fact, that a display of emotion on his part seemed out of place. Her tone was casual, her clasped hands still, her eyes unflinching. She did not ask for pity, she never had. The next remark she made was about their Indian summer.

'I'm sorry,' Bartholomew said.

He didn't know her: that thought came, which never had before. Her severity, the outspokenness that was natural to her, told too little. She had saved him from Sally Carbery, she would have said, believing that was the honest way to put it. He'd known in childhood that she wasn't liked. He had tried to make it up to her, and was glad now that he had.

But shadowing these reflections, and belittling them, was what Hester bore so stocially. It stalked the past, and was in charge of all time that now was left. And yet, for Bartholomew, his own trouble was the greater agony; he could not help it that this was so and in a familiar manner guilt began. That day he did more in the house, taking on his sister's tasks.

*

'What courage you have!' Bartholomew said when autumn had passed, and winter too.

Hester shook her head. Courage came with misfortune; she took no credit for it. She asked for primroses and watched while Bartholomew picked them from the bank where they grew. That night they were on her bedside table, in a glass there'd been at Maunder Street.

'Why did they give me that awful name?' she asked when Bartholomew came to her later, to say goodnight. The name had come from somewhere outside the family; she wondered where. When Bartholomew was born they said it was the day the Huguenots had been slaughtered in France.

'I've brought you Ovaltine,' he said.

It made her sleep, or was supposed to, but when he came with tea in the mornings he didn't ask if she had lain awake. The nights were long. He brought the tea as early as he could.

On Sundays she could no longer manage the journey to church; but messages came from the Oscarey parishioners, prayers were said for her. 'O, Lord,' she imagined Bartholomew pleading on her behalf, 'look down from heaven, and relieve Thy servant . . . Look down upon her with the eyes of Thy mercy . . . give her comfort and sure confidence in Thee . . .'

This was the form she preferred; and she knew as she lay in her bed in the stillness of the rectory that these were the words said.

*

Bartholomew wondered if, afterwards, he would want to go away; if, without her, his own misfortune would be a desolation he could not bear. Back to the northside, he thought, which he knew better than the rest of Dublin. There would be employment of some kind; of any kind, he didn't much mind what, provided only that he was capable of whatever it was. He wondered about helping in one of the shops or a bed-and-breakfast house. Middle-aged now, the youths he had worked among might be able at least to find him something, if not to employ him. And yet it seemed ridiculous that he should even consider such a dramatic move. He knew he would remain, and be silent.

'How tidy it is!' Hester murmured. 'Living for your while, then not being there any more. How well arranged!'

There was contentment in how she put it, and in her tone. Bartholomew sensed that and, concerned with her again, rather than with himself, he was pleased. His deception of her and of his scanty congregations would one day assault his conscience, would one day make continuing impossible, but at least she would not have to know.

*

When the time came, Hester knew that she would die that night.

Bartholomew was with her. There was no sentiment, she didn't speak, and Bartholomew sensed that there suddenly was only pain. God's will, he knew, was what she repeated to herself, as she had since she'd realized her illness was a visitation that would only end as it was ending now. The intensity of her faith, the sureness of her trust, was unaffected by the pain she suffered, and he prayed that she would close her eyes and die. Yet she did not, and Bartholomew telephoned to request that more morphine should be brought.

'No, I can manage,' she whispered, hearing this plea, although he had made it in another room. No doctor was available; a message had had to be left. 'Soon,' Hester said, her voice just audible, no more. 'It will be soon.' She asked for Communion then.

Outside, a frost had stayed all that day and, icing over now, still whitened the small garden, the patch of grass, the fields beyond. Bartholomew stood by the window, watching another dusk becoming dark, wishing there was not now, unknown to her, a gulf between them. Her courage was her belief, a dignity in her need, her eternal life already lit, its stately angels waiting to take her to the mansions of their paradise, and choral voices singing.

When Bartholomew returned to the bedside she was quiet. Then she spoke incomprehensibly. She winced, her closed eyes tightening, her head jerking on the pillow; and he went again to the telephone. 'Please,' he begged. 'Please.' But there was still a message. He said a little more, whispering now, the desperation in his voice concealed. Outside, a blackbird, tame in the garden, scratched at the frost.

'Hester,' he said, again beside her, and there was no response; he had not expected one. She would die and still be here and nowhere else: in his dissent he could not escape that. 'There will be nothing,' he might have said, and wanted to share with her his anguish, as she shared the ordeal of death with him.

'Hester,' he murmured.

She turned away, shuddering off a convulsion as best she could, but another came and she was restless. Confused, she tried to sit up and he eased her back to the pillows. For a moment then her eyes were clear, her contorted features loosened and were calm. Bartholomew knew that pain was taken from her and that she shed, in this first moment of her eternity, her too-long, gnawing discontent; that peace, elusive for a lifetime, had come at last.

He reached out for her hand and felt it warm in his. 'Thank you,' he thought she said, but knew she had not. He gazed for a little longer at the dead features before he drew the sheet up.

He made the telephone calls that were necessary, cancelling the message that requested morphine, informing an undertaker. He tidied the room, clearing away medicine, a cup and saucer.

He sat downstairs, close to the fire, for it was colder now. He remembered days there had been, and Maunder Street, the games they played in the backyard, the afternoon Hester took him into the Botanic Gardens, another time to see a band going by in the streets.

Bartholomew watched the fire become embers, not taking anything to eat, disturbed by no one. That night he slept fitfully and woke often, his sister's death entangled in his dreams with his own deprivation. He woke often, and soon after dawn he went to Hester's room.

When he drew down the sheet the moment of calm was still caught in her features. He stayed with her, the mercy of her tranquillity seeming to be a miracle that was real, as it had been in the instant of death. Heaven enough, and more than angels.

# Folie à Deux

Aware of a presence close to him, Wilby glances up from the book he has just begun to read. The man standing there says nothing. He doesn't smile. A dishcloth hangs from where it's tucked into grubby apron-strings knotted at the front, and Wilby assumes that the man is an envoy sent from the kitchen to apologize for the delay in the cooking of the fish he has ordered.

The place is modest, in rue Piques off rue de Sèvres: Wilby didn't notice what it is called. A café as much as a brasserie, it is poorly illuminated except for the bar, at which a couple are hunched over their glasses, conversing softly. One of the few tables belonging to the café is occupied by four elderly women playing cards and there are a few people at tables in the brasserie.

Still without communicating, the man who has come from the kitchen turns and goes away, leaving Wilby with the impression that he has been mistaken for someone else. He pours himself more wine and reads again. Wilby reads a lot, and drinks a lot.

He is a spare, sharp-faced man in his forties, clean-shaven, in a grey suit, with a striped blue-and-red tie almost but not quite striking a stylish note. He visits Paris once in a while to make the rounds of salerooms specializing in rare postage stamps, usually spinning out his time when he is there, since he can afford to. Three years ago he inherited his family's wine business in County Westmeath, which he sold eighteen months later, planning to live on the proceeds while he indulged his interest in philately. He occupies, alone now, the house he inherited at that time also, creeper-clad, just outside the Westmeath town where he was born. Marriage failed him there, or he it, and he doubts that he will make another attempt in that direction.

His food is brought to him by a small, old waiter, a more presentable figure than the man who came and went. He is attentive, addressing Wilby in conventional waiter's terms and supplying, when they are asked for, salt and pepper from another table. '*Voilà, monsieur*,' he murmurs, his tone apologetic.

Wilby eats his fish, wondering what fish it is. He knew when he ordered it but has since forgotten, and the taste doesn't tell him much. The bread is the best part of his meal and he catches the waiter's attention to ask for more. His book is a paperback he has read before, *The Hand of Ethelberta*.

He reads another page, orders more wine, finishes the *pommes frites* but not the fish. He likes quiet places, and doesn't hurry. He orders coffee and – though not intending to – a calvados. He drinks too much, he tells himself, and restrains the inclination to have another when the coffee comes. He reads again, indulging the pleasure of being in Paris, in a brasserie where Muzak isn't playing, at a small corner table, engrossed in a story that's familiar yet has receded sufficiently to be blurred in places, like something good remembered. He never minds it when the food isn't up to much; wine matters more, and peace. He'll walk back to the Hôtel Merneuil; with luck he'll be successful in the salerooms tomorrow.

He gestures for his bill, and pays. The old waiter has his overcoat ready for him at the door, and Wilby tips him a little for that. Outside, being late November, the night is chilly.

The man who came to look at him is there on the street, dressed as he was then. He stands still, not speaking. He might have come outside to have a cigarette, as waiters sometimes do. But there is no cigarette.

'*Bonsoir*,' Wilby says.

'*Bonsoir*.'

Saying that, quite suddenly the man is someone else. A resemblance flickers: the smooth black hair, the head like the rounded end of a bullet, the fringe that is not as once it was but is still a fringe, the dark eyes. There is a way of standing, without unease or agitation and yet awkward, hands lank, open.

'What is all this?' Even as he puts the question, Wilby's choice of words sounds absurd to him. 'Anthony?' he says.

There is a movement, a hand's half gesture, meaningless, hardly a response. Then the man turns away, entering the brasserie by another door.

'Anthony,' Wilby mutters again, but only to himself.

People have said that Anthony is dead.

\*

The streets are emptier than they were, the bustle of the pavements gone. Obedient to pedestrian lights at rue de Babylone where there is fast-moving traffic again, Wilby waits with a woman in a pale waterproof coat, her legs slim beneath it, blonde hair brushed up. Not wanting to think about Anthony, he wonders if she's a tart, since she has that look, and for a moment sees her pale coat thrown down in some small room, the glow of an electric fire, money placed on a dressing-table: now and again when he travels he has a woman. But this one doesn't glance at him, and the red light changes to green.

It couldn't possibly have been Anthony, of course it couldn't. Even assuming that Anthony is alive, why would he be employed as a kitchen worker in Paris? 'Yes, I'm afraid we fear the worst,' his father said on the telephone, years ago now. 'He sent a few belongings here, but that's a good while back. A note to you, unfinished, was caught up in the pages of a book. Nothing in it, really. Your name, no more.'

In rue du Bac there is a window Wilby likes, with prints of the Revolution. The display has hardly changed since he was here last: the death of Marie Antoinette, the Girondists on their way to the guillotine, the storming of the Bastille, Danton's death, Robespierre triumphant, Robespierre fallen from grace. Details aren't easy to make out in the dim street-light. Prints he hasn't seen before are indistinguishable at the back.

At a bar he has another calvados. He said himself when people asked him – a few had once – that he, too, imagined Anthony was dead. A disappearance so prolonged, with no reports of even a glimpse as the years advanced, did appear to confirm a conclusion that became less tentative, and in the end wasn't tentative at all.

In rue Montalembert a couple ask for directions to the Métro. Wilby points it out, walking back a little way with them to do so, as grateful for this interruption as he was when the woman at the traffic crossing caught his interest.

'*Bonne nuit, monsieur.*' In the hall of the Hôtel Merneuil the night porter holds open the lift doors. He closes them and the lift begins its smooth ascent. 'The will to go on can fall away, you know,' Anthony's father said on the telephone again, in touch to find out if there was anything to report.

*

Monsieur Jothy shakes his head over the pay packet that hasn't been picked up. It's on the windowsill above the sinks, where others have been ignored too. He writes a message on it and props it against an empty bottle.

At this late hour Monsieur Jothy has the kitchen to himself, a time for assessing what needs to be ordered, for satisfying himself that, in general, the kitchen is managing. He picks up Jean-André's note of what he particularly requires for tomorrow, and checks the shelves where the cleaning materials are kept. He has recently become suspicious of Jean-André, suspecting short-cuts. His risotto, once an attraction on the menu, is scarcely ever ordered now; and with reason in Monsieur Jothy's opinion, since it has lost the intensity of flavour that made it popular, and is often dry. But the kitchen at least is clean, and Monsieur Jothy, examining cutlery and plates, fails to find food clinging anywhere, or a rim left on a cup. Once he employed two dish-washers at the sinks, but now one does it on his own, and half the time forgets his wages. Anxious to keep him, Monsieur Jothy has wondered about finding somewhere for him to sleep on the premises instead of having the long journey to and from his room. But there isn't even a corner of a pantry, and when he asked in the neighbour-hood about accommodation near rue Piques he was also unsuccessful.

The dishcloths, washed and rinsed, are draped on the radiators and will be dry by the morning, the soup bowls are stacked; the glasses, in their rows, gleam on the side table. '*Très bon, très bon,*' Monsieur Jothy murmurs before he turns the lights out and locks up.

\*

Wilby does not sleep and cannot read, although he tries to.

'A marvel, isn't it?' Miss Davally said, the memory vivid, as if she'd said it yesterday. You wouldn't think apricots would so easily ripen in such a climate. Even on a wall lined with brick you wouldn't think it. She pointed at the branches sprawled out along their wires, and you could see the fruit in little clusters. 'Delphiniums,' she said, pointing again, and one after another named the flowers they passed on their way through the garden. 'And this is Anthony,' she said in the house.

The boy looked up from the playing cards he had spread out on the floor. 'What's his name?' he asked, and Miss Davally said he knew because she had told him already. But even so she did so again. 'Why's he called that?' Anthony asked. 'Why're you called that?'

'It's my name.'

'Shall we play in the garden?'

That first day, and every day afterwards, there were gingersnap biscuits in the middle of the morning. 'Am I older than you?' Anthony asked. 'Is six older?' He had a house, he said, in the bushes at the end of the garden, and they pretended there was a house. 'Jericho he's called,' Anthony said of the dog that followed them about, a black Labrador with an injured leg that hung limply, thirteen years old. 'Miss Davally is an orphan,' Anthony said. 'That's why she lives with us. Do you know what an orphan is?'

In the yard the horses looked out over the half-doors of their stables; the hounds were in a smaller yard. Anthony's mother was never at lunch because her horse and the hounds were exercised then. But his father always was, each time wearing a different tweed jacket, his grey moustache clipped short, the olives he liked to see on the lunch table always there, the whiskey he took for his health. 'Well, young chap, how are you?' he always asked.

On wet days they played marbles in the kitchen passages, the dog stretched out beside them. 'You come to the sea in summer,' Anthony said. 'They told me.' Every

July: the long journey from Westmeath to the same holiday cottage on the cliffs above the bay that didn't have a name. It was Miss Davally who had told Anthony all that, and in time – so that hospitality might be returned – she often drove Anthony there and back. An outing for her too, she used to say, and sometimes she brought a cake she'd made, being in the way of bringing a present when she went to people's houses. She liked it at the sea as much as Anthony did; she liked to turn the wheel of the bellows in the kitchen of the cottage and watch the sparks flying up; and Anthony liked the hard sand of the shore, and collecting flintstones, and netting shrimps. The dog prowled about the rocks, sniffing the seaweed, clawing at the sea-anemones. 'Our house,' Anthony called the cave they found when they crawled through an opening in the rocks, a cave no one knew was there.

\*

Air from the window Wilby slightly opens at the top is refreshing and brings with it, for a moment, the chiming of two o'clock. His book is open, face downward to keep his place, his bedside light still on. But the dark is better, and he extinguishes it.

There was a blue vase in the recess of the staircase wall, nothing else there; and paperweights crowded the shallow landing shelves, all touching one another; forty-six, Anthony said. His mother played the piano in the drawing-room. 'Hullo,' she said, holding out her hand and smiling. She wasn't much like someone who exercised foxhounds: slim and small and wearing scent, she was also beautiful. 'Look!' Anthony said, pointing at the lady in the painting above the mantelpiece in the hall.

Miss Davally was a distant relative as well as being an orphan, and when she sat on the sands after her bathe she often talked about her own childhood in the house where she'd been given a home: how a particularly unpleasant boy used to creep up on her and pull a cracker in her ear, how she hated her ribboned pigtails and persuaded a simple-minded maid to cut them off, how she taught the kitchen cat to dance and how people said they'd never seen the like.

Every lunchtime Anthony's father kept going a conversation about a world that was not yet known to his listeners. He spoke affectionately of the playboy pugilist Jack Doyle, demonstrating the subtlety of his right punch and recalling the wonders of his hell-raising before poverty claimed him. He told of the exploits of an ingenious escapologist, Major Pat Reid. He condemned the first Earl of Inchiquin as the most disgraceful man ever to step out of Ireland.

Much other information was passed on at the lunch table: why aeroplanes flew, how clocks kept time, why spiders spun their webs and how they did it. Information was everything, Anthony's father maintained, and its lunchtime dissemination, with Miss Davally's reminiscences, nurtured curiosity: the unknown became a fascination. 'What would happen if you didn't eat?' Anthony wondered; and there were attempts to see if it was possible to create a rainbow with a water hose when the sun was bright, and the discovery made that, in fact, it was. A jellyfish was scooped into a shrimp net to see if it would perish or survive when it was tipped out on to the sand. Miss Davally said to put it back, and warned that jellyfish could sting as terribly as wasps.

A friendship developed between Miss Davally and Wilby's mother – a formal association, first names not called upon, neither in conversation nor in the letters that came to be exchanged from one summer to the next. *Anthony is said to be clever*, Miss Davally's spidery handwriting told. And then, as if that perhaps required watering down, *Well, so they say*. It was reported also that when each July drew near Anthony began to count the days. *He values the friendship so!* Miss Davally commented. *How fortunate for two only children such a friendship is!*

Fortunate indeed it seemed to be. There was no quarrelling, no vying for authority, no competing. When, one summer, a yellow Lilo was washed up, still inflated, it was taken to the cave that no one else knew about, neither claiming that it was his because he'd seen it first. 'Someone lost that thing,' Anthony said, but no one came looking for it. They didn't know what it was, only that it floated. They floated it themselves, the dog limping behind them when they carried it to the sea, his tail wagging madly, head cocked to one side. In the cave it became a bed for him, to clamber on to when he was tired.

The Lilo was another of the friendship's precious secrets, as the cave itself was. No other purpose was found for it, but its possession was enough to make it the highlight of that particular summer and on the last day of July it was again carried to the edge of the sea. 'Now, now,' the dog was calmed when he became excited. The waves that morning were hardly waves at all.

*

In the dark there is a pinprick glow of red somewhere on the television set. The air that comes into the room is colder and Wilby closes the window he has opened a crack, suppressing the murmur of a distant plane. Memory won't let him go now; he knows it won't and makes no effort to resist it.

Nothing was said when they watched the drowning of the dog. Old Jericho was clever, never at a loss when there was fun. Not moving, he was obedient, as he always was. He played his part, going with the Lilo when it floated out, a deep black shadow, sharp against the garish yellow. They watched as they had watched the hosepipe rainbow gathering colour, as Miss Davally said she'd watched the shaky steps of the dancing cat. Far away already, the yellow of the Lilo became a blur on the water, was lost, was there again and lost again, and the barking began, and became a wail. Nothing was said then either. Nor when they climbered over the shingle and the rocks, and climbed up to the short-cut and passed through the gorse field. From the cliff they looked again, for the last time, far out to the horizon. The sea was undisturbed, glittering in the sunlight. 'So what have you two been up to this morning?' Miss Davally asked. The next day, somewhere else, the dog was washed in.

Miss Davally blamed herself, for that was in her nature. But she could not be blamed. It was agreed that she could not be. Unaware of his limitations – more than a little blind, with only three active legs – old Jericho had had a way of going into the sea when he sensed a piece of driftwood bobbing about. Once too often he had done that. His grave was in the garden, a small slate plaque let into the turf, his name and dates.

They did not ever speak to one another about the drowning of the dog. They did not ever say they had not meant it to occur. There was no blame, no accusing. They had not called it a game, only said they wondered what would happen, what the dog would do. The silence had begun before they pushed the Lilo out.

Other summers brought other incidents, other experiences, but there was no such occurrence again. There were adjustments in the friendship, since passing time demanded that, and different games were played, and there were different conversations, and new discoveries.

Then, one winter, a letter from Miss Davally was less cheerful than her letters usually were. *Withdrawn*, she wrote, *and they are concerned*. What she declared, in detail after that, was confirmed when summer came: Anthony was different, and more different still in later summers, quieter, timid, seeming sometimes to be lost. It was a mystery when the dog's gravestone disappeared from the garden.

\*

In the dark, the bright red dot of the television light still piercingly there, Wilby wonders, as so often he has, what influence there was when without incitement or persuasion, without words, they did what had been done. They were nine years old then, when secrets became deception.

It was snowing the evening he and Anthony met again, both of them waiting in the chapel cloisters for their names, as new boys, to be called out. It was not a surprise that Anthony was there, passing on from the school that years ago had declared him clever; nor was it by chance that they were to be together for what remained of their education. 'Nice for Anthony to have someone he knows,' his father said on the telephone, and confirmed that Anthony was still as he had become.

In the dim evening light the snow blew softly into the cloisters, and when the roll-call ended and a noisy dispersal began, the solitary figure remained, the same smooth black hair, a way of standing that hadn't changed. 'How are you?' Wilby asked. His friend's smile, once so readily there, came as a shadow and then was lost in awkwardness.

Peculiar, Anthony was called at school, but wasn't bullied, as though it had been realized that bullying would yield no satisfaction. He lacked skill at games, avoided all pursuits that were not compulsory, displayed immediate evidence of his cleverness, science and mathematical subjects his forte. Religious boys attempted to befriend him, believing that to be a duty; kindly masters sought to draw him out. 'Well, yes, I knew him,' Wilby admitted, lamely explaining his association with someone who was so very much not like the friends he made now. 'A long time ago,' he nearly always added.

Passing by the windows of empty classrooms, he several times noticed Anthony, the only figure among the unoccupied desks. And often – on the drive that ended at the school gates, or often anywhere – there was the same lone figure in the distance. On the golf-course where senior boys were allowed to play, Anthony sometimes sat on a seat against a wall, watching the golfers as they approached, watching them as they walked on. He shied away when conversation threatened, creeping back into his shadowlands.

One day he wasn't there, his books left tidily in his desk, clothes hanging in his dormitory locker, his pyjamas under his pillow. He would be on his way home, since boys who kept themselves to themselves were often homesick. But he had not attempted to go home and was found still within the school grounds, having broken no rules except that he had ignored for a day the summoning of bells.

\*

Dawn comes darkly, and Wilby sleeps. But his sleep is brief, his dreams forgotten when he wakes. The burden of guilt that came when in silence they clambered over the shingle and the rocks, when they passed through the gorse field, was muddled by bewilderment, a child's tormenting panic not yet constrained by suppression as later it would be. Long afterwards, when first he heard that Anthony was dead – and when he said it himself – the remnants of the shame guilt had become fell away.

He shaves and washes, dresses slowly. In the hall the reception clerks have just come on duty. They nod at him, wish him good-day. No call this morning for an umbrella, one says.

Outside it is not entirely day, or even day at all. The cleaning lorries are on the streets, water pouring in the gutters, but there's no one about in rue du Bac, refuse sacks still waiting to be collected. A bar is open further on, men standing at the counter, disinclined for conversation with one another. A sleeping figure in a doorway has not been roused. What hovel, Wilby wonders as he passes, does a kitchen worker occupy?

In rue Piques the brasserie is shuttered, no lights showing anywhere. Cardboard boxes are stacked close to the glass of three upstairs windows, others are uncurtained; none suggests the domesticity of a dwelling. Le Père Jothy the place is called.

Wilby roams the nearby streets. A few more cafés are opening and in one coffee is brought to him. He sips it, breaking a croissant. There's no one else, except the barman.

He knows he should go away. He should take the train to Passy, to the salerooms he has planned to visit there; he should not ever return to rue Piques. He has lived easily with an aberration, then shaken it off: what happened was almost nothing.

Other men come in, a woman on her own, her face

bruised on one side, no effort made to conceal the darkening weals. Her voice is low when she explains this injury to the barman, her fingers now and again touching it. Soundlessly, she weeps when she has taken her cognac to a table.

Oh, this is silly! his unspoken comment was when Miss Davally's letter came, its implications apparent only to him. For heaven's sake! he crossly muttered, the words kept to himself when he greeted Anthony in the cloisters, and again every time he caught sight of him on the golf-course. The old dog's life had been all but over. And Wilby remembers now – as harshly as he has in the night – the bitterness of his resentment when a friendship he delighted in was destroyed, when Anthony's world – the garden, the house, his mother, his father, Miss Davally – was no longer there.

'He has no use for us,' his father said. 'No use for anyone, we think.'

\*

Turning into rue Piques, Anthony notices at once the figure waiting outside the ribbon shop. It is November the twenty-fourth, the last Thursday of the month. This day won't come again.

'*Bonjour*,' he says.

'How are you, Anthony?'

And Anthony says that Monday is the closed day. Not that Sunday isn't too. If someone waited outside the ribbon shop on a Monday or a Sunday it wouldn't be much good. Not that many people wait there.

Wind blows a scrap of paper about, close to where they stand. In the window of the ribbon shop coils of ribbon are in all widths and colours, and there are swatches of trimming for other purposes, lace and velvet, and plain white edging, and a display of button cards. Anthony often looks to see if there has been a change, but there never has been.

'How are you, Anthony?'

It is a fragment of a white paper bag that is blown about and Anthony identifies it from the remains of the red script that advertises the *boulangerie* in rue Dupin. When it is blown closer to him he catches it under his shoe.

'People have wondered where you are, Anthony.'

'I went away from Ireland.'

Anthony bends and picks up the litter he has trapped. He says he has the ovens to do today. A Thursday, and he works in the morning.

'Miss Davally still writes, wondering if there is news of you.'

Half past eight is his time on Thursdays. Anthony says that, and adds that there's never a complaint in the kitchen. One speck on the prong of a fork could lead to a complaint, a shred of fish skin could, a cabbage leaf. But there's never a complaint.

'People thought you were dead, Anthony.'

\*

Wilby says he sold the wineshop. He described it once, when they were children: the shelves of bottles, the different shapes, their contents red or white, pink if people wanted that. He tasted wine a few times, he remembers saying.

'Your father has died himself, Anthony. Your mother has. Miss Davally was left the house because there was no one else. She lives there now.'

No response comes; Wilby has not expected one. He has become a philatelist, he says.

*

Anthony nods, waiting to cross the street. He knows his father died, his mother too. He has guessed Miss Davally inherited the house. The deaths were in the *Irish Times*, which he always read, cover to cover, all the years he was the night porter at the Cliff Castle Hotel in Dalkey.

He doesn't mention the Cliff Castle Hotel. He doesn't say he misses the *Irish Times*, the familiar names, the political news, the photographs of places, the change there is in Ireland now. *Le Monde* is more staid, more circumspect, more serious. Anthony doesn't say that either because he doubts that it's of interest to a visitor to Paris.

A gap comes in the stream of cars that has begun to go by; but not trusting this opportunity, Anthony still waits. He is careful on the streets, even though he knows them well.

'I haven't died,' he says.

*

Perfectly together, they shared an act that was too shameful to commit alone, taking a chance on a sunny morning in order to discover if an old dog's cleverness would see to his survival.

For a moment, while Anthony loses another opportunity to cross the street, Wilby gathers into sentences how he might attempt a denial that this was how it was, how best to put it differently. An accident, a misfortune beyond anticipation, the unexpected: with gentleness, for gentleness is due, he is about to plead. But Anthony crosses the street then, and opens with a key the side door of the brasserie. He makes no gesture of farewell, he does not look back.

*

Walking by the river on his way to the salerooms at Passy, Wilby wishes he'd said he was glad his friend was not dead. It is his only thought. The pleasure-boats slip by on the water beside him, hardly anyone on them. A child waves. Raised too late in response, Wilby's own hand drops to his side. The wind that blew the litter about in rue Piques has freshened. It snatches at the remaining leaves on the black-trunked trees that are an orderly line, following the river's course.

The salerooms are on the other bank, near the radio building and the apartment block that change the river's character. Several times he has visited this vast display in which the world's stamps are exhibited behind glass if they are notably valuable, on the tables, country by country, when they are not. That busy image has always excited Wilby's imagination and as he climbs the steps to the bridge he is near he attempts to anticipate it now, but does not entirely succeed.

It is not in punishment that the ovens are cleaned on another Thursday morning. It is not in expiation that soon the first leavings of the day will be scraped from the lunchtime plates. There is no bothering with redemption. Looking down from the bridge at the sluggish flow of water, Wilby confidently asserts that. A morning murkiness, like dusk, has brought some lights on in the apartment block. Traffic crawls on distant streets.

For Anthony, the betrayal matters, the folly, the carelessness that would have been forgiven, the cruelty. It mattered in the silence – while they watched, while they clambered over the shingle and the rocks, while they passed through the gorse field. It matters now. The haunted sea is all the truth there is for Anthony, what he honours because it matters still.

The buyers move among the tables and Wilby knows that for him, in this safe, second-hand world of postage stamps, tranquillity will return. He knows where he is with all this; he knows what he's about, as he does in other aspects of his tidy life. And yet this morning he likes himself less than he likes his friend.

# He just wanted a decent book to read ...

Not too much to ask, is it? It was in 1935 when Allen Lane, Managing Director of Bodley Head Publishers, stood on a platform at Exeter railway station looking for something good to read on his journey back to London. His choice was limited to popular magazines and poor-quality paperbacks – the same choice faced every day by the vast majority of readers, few of whom could afford hardbacks. Lane's disappointment and subsequent anger at the range of books generally available led him to found a company – and change the world.

*'We believed in the existence in this country of a vast reading public for intelligent books at a low price, and staked everything on it'*
**Sir Allen Lane, 1902–1970, founder of Penguin Books**

The quality paperback had arrived – and not just in bookshops. Lane was adamant that his Penguins should appear in chain stores and tobacconists, and should cost no more than a packet of cigarettes.

Reading habits (and cigarette prices) have changed since 1935, but Penguin still believes in publishing the best books for everybody to enjoy. We still believe that good design costs no more than bad design, and we still believe that quality books published passionately and responsibly make the world a better place.

So wherever you see the little bird – whether it's on a piece of prize-winning literary fiction or a celebrity autobiography, political tour de force or historical masterpiece, a serial-killer thriller, reference book, world classic or a piece of pure escapism – you can bet that it represents the very best that the genre has to offer.

**Whatever you like to read – trust Penguin.**

read more
www.penguin.co.uk